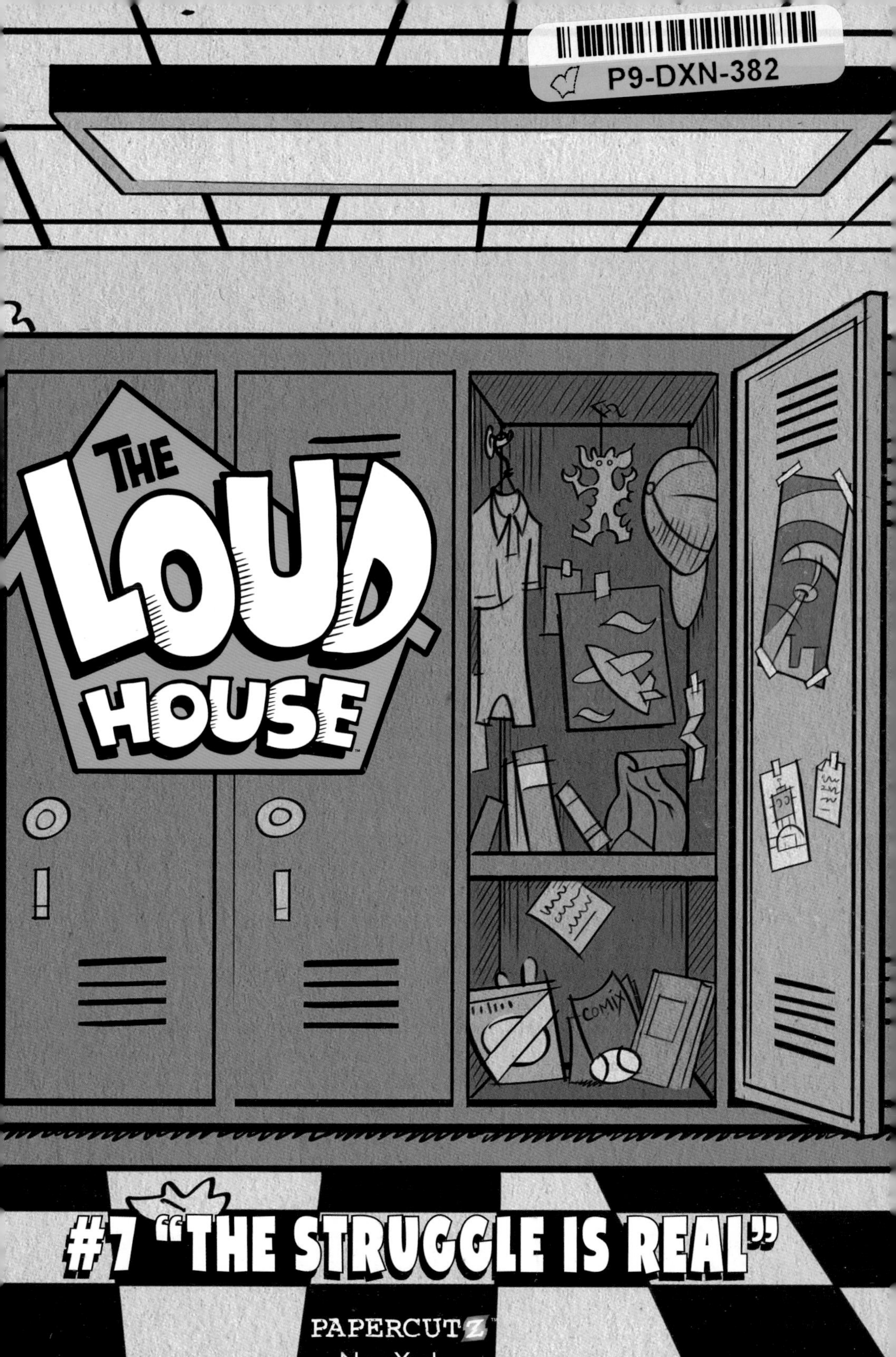
COMIX

THE LOUD HOUSE

#7 "THE STRUGGLE IS REAL"

PAPERCUTZ
New York

nickelodeon GRAPHIC NOVELS AVAILABLE FROM PAPERCUTZ

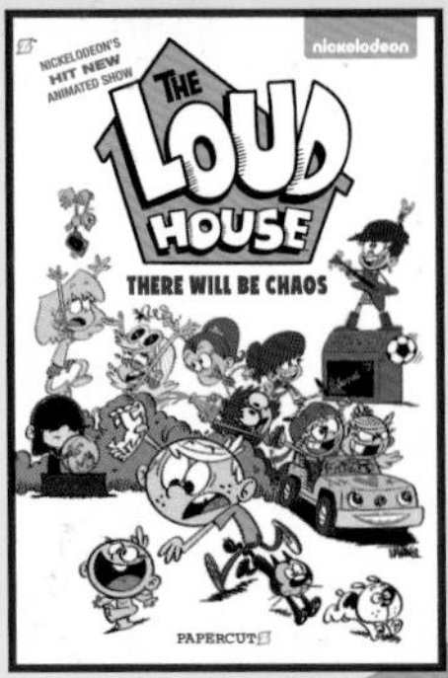
NICKELODEON'S HIT NEW ANIMATED SHOW
nickelodeon
THE LOUD HOUSE
THERE WILL BE CHAOS
PAPERCUTZ

THE LOUD HOUSE
#1
"There Will Be Chaos"

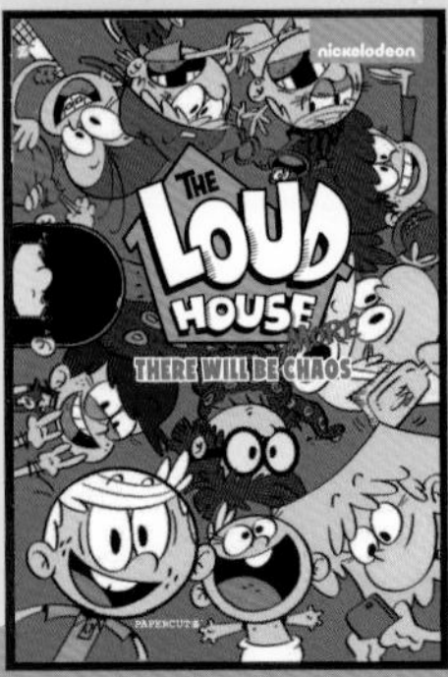
nickelodeon
THE LOUD HOUSE
THERE WILL BE CHAOS
PAPERCUTZ

THE LOUD HOUSE
#2
"There Will Be More Chaos"

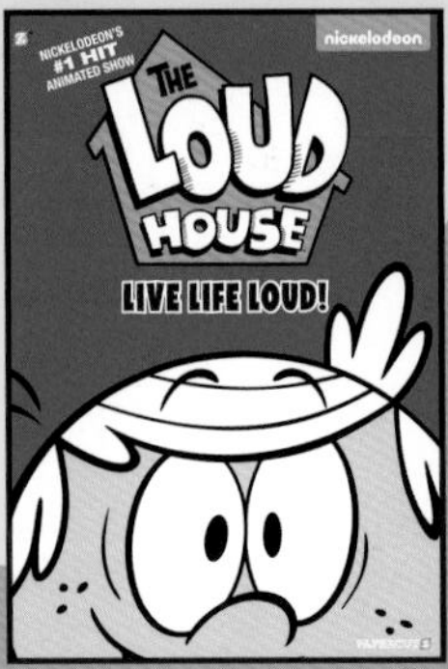
NICKELODEON'S #1 HIT ANIMATED SHOW
nickelodeon
THE LOUD HOUSE
LIVE LIFE LOUD!
PAPERCUTZ

THE LOUD HOUSE
#3
"Live Life Loud!"

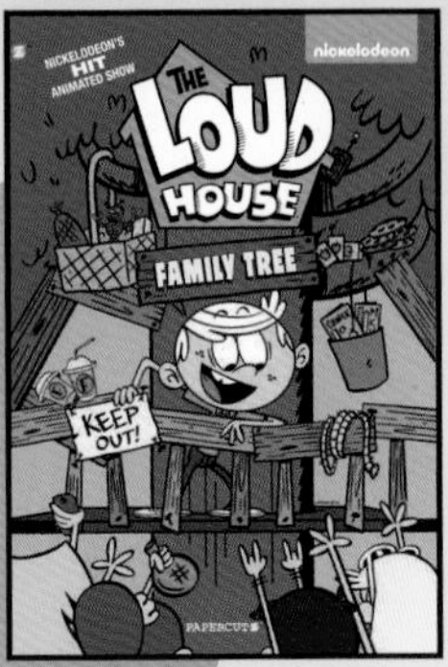
NICKELODEON'S HIT ANIMATED SHOW
nickelodeon
THE LOUD HOUSE
FAMILY TREE
KEEP OUT!
PAPERCUTZ

THE LOUD HOUSE
#4
"Family Tree"

COMING SOON

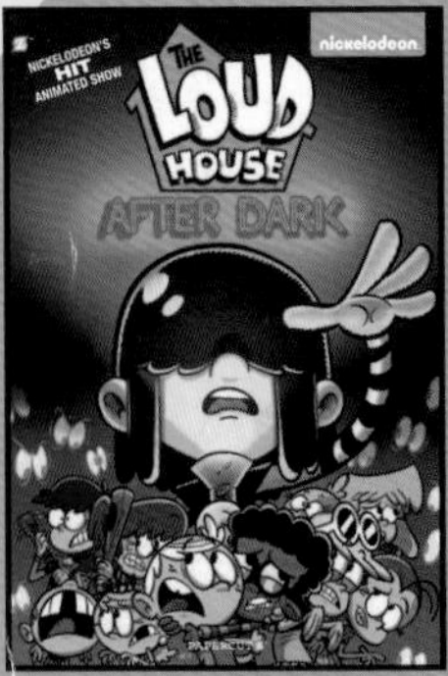
NICKELODEON'S HIT ANIMATED SHOW
nickelodeon
THE LOUD HOUSE
AFTER DARK
PAPERCUTZ

THE LOUD HOUSE
#5
"After Dark"

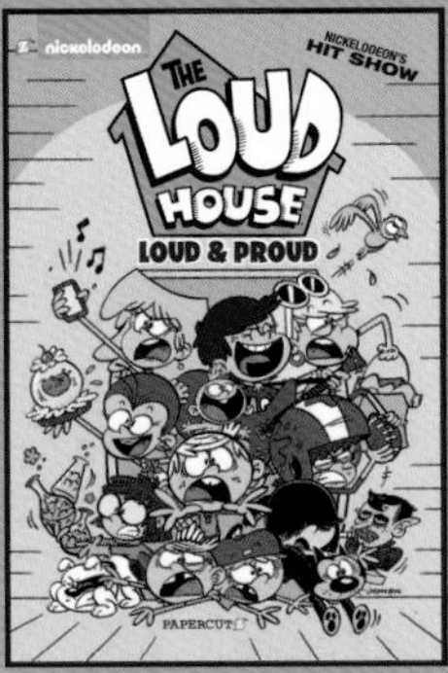
nickelodeon
NICKELODEON'S HIT SHOW
THE LOUD HOUSE
LOUD & PROUD
PAPERCUTZ

THE LOUD HOUSE
#6
"Loud and Proud"

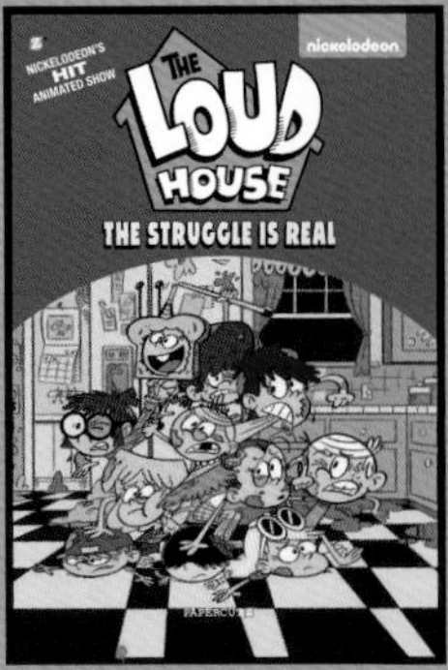
NICKELODEON'S HIT ANIMATED SHOW
nickelodeon
THE LOUD HOUSE
THE STRUGGLE IS REAL
PAPERCUTZ

THE LOUD HOUSE
#7
"The Struggle is Real"

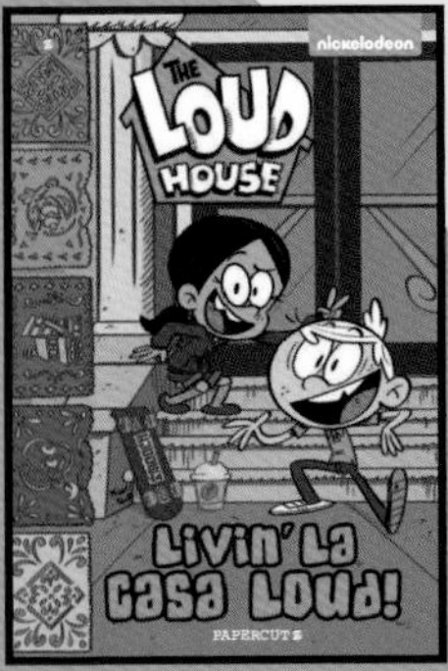
nickelodeon
THE LOUD HOUSE
Livin' La Casa Loud!
PAPERCUTZ

THE LOUD HOUSE
#8
"Livin' La Casa Loud"

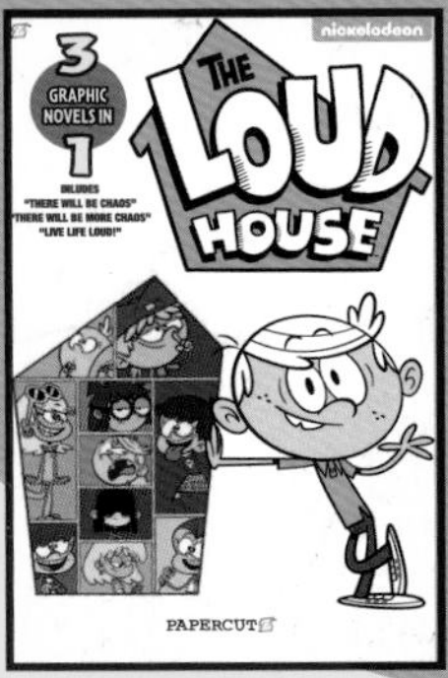
nickelodeon
3 GRAPHIC NOVELS IN 1
INCLUDES "THERE WILL BE CHAOS" "THERE WILL BE MORE CHAOS" "LIVE LIFE LOUD!"
THE LOUD HOUSE
PAPERCUTZ

THE LOUD HOUSE
3 IN 1
#1

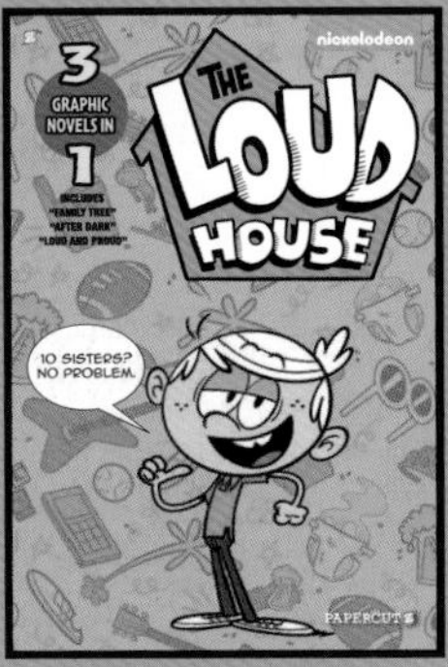
nickelodeon
3 GRAPHIC NOVELS IN 1
INCLUDES "FAMILY TREE" "AFTER DARK" "LOUD AND PROUD"
THE LOUD HOUSE
10 SISTERS? NO PROBLEM.
PAPERCUTZ

THE LOUD HOUSE
3 IN 1
#2

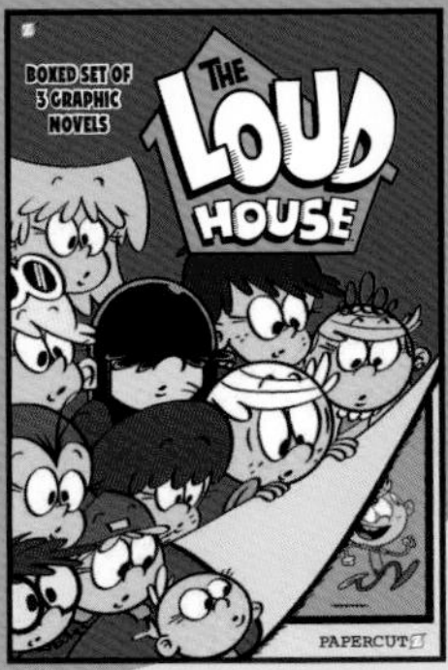
BOXED SET OF 3 GRAPHIC NOVELS
THE LOUD HOUSE
PAPERCUTZ

THE LOUD HOUSE
BOXED SET
$23.99

LOUD HOUSE graphic novels are available for $7.99 each in paperback, $12.99 each in hardcover. LOUD HOUSE 3 IN 1 is available for $14.99 each in hardcover only. THE LOUD HOUSE BOXED SET is available for $23.99. Available from booksellers everywhere. You can also order online from Papercutz.com, or call 1-800-886-1223, Monday through Friday, 9-5 EST. MC, Visa, and AmEx accepted. To order by mail, please add $5.00 for postage and handling for the first book ordered, $1.00 for each additional book and make check payable to NBM Publishing.
Send to: Papercutz, 160 Broadway, Suite 700, East Wing, New York, NY 10038.

THE LOUD HOUSE

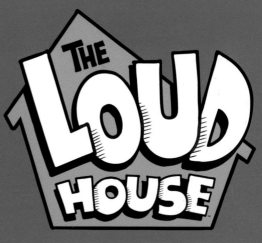

#7 "THE STRUGGLE IS REAL"

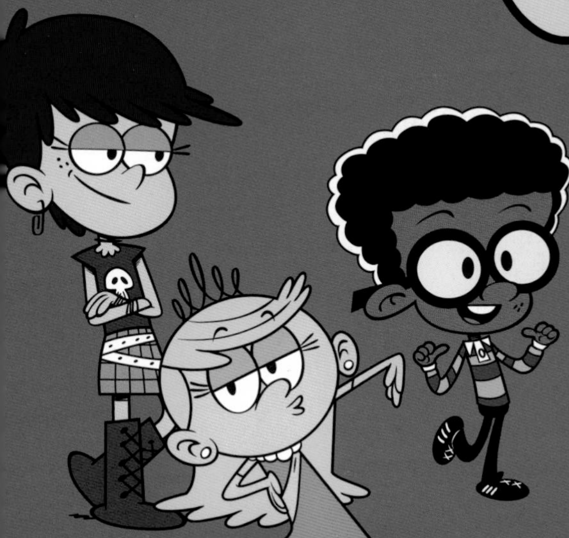

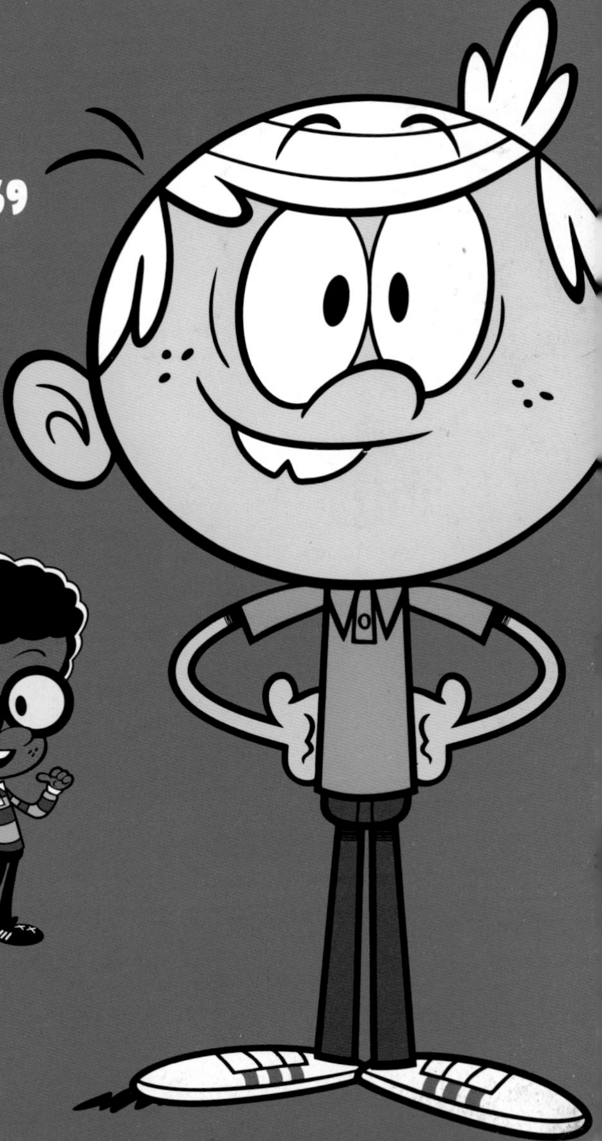

nickelodeon THE LOUD HOUSE #7 "THE STRUGGLE IS REAL"

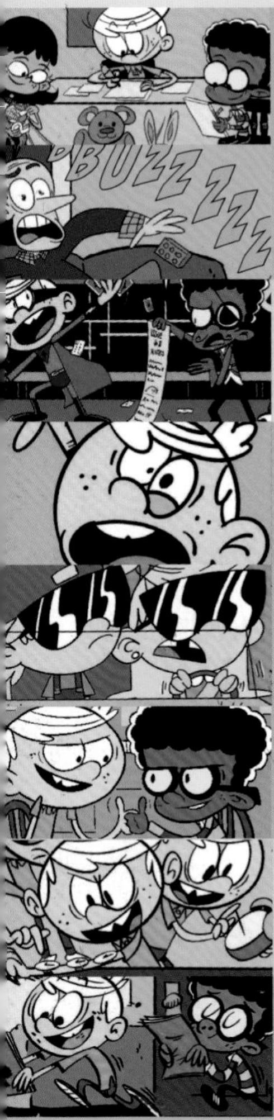
BUZZ

"BUSINESS CENTS"
Angela Entzminger—Writer, Artist
Ronda Pattison—Colorist
Wilson Ramos Jr.—Letterer

"PREP TALK"
Derek Fridolfs—Writer
Angela Zhang—Artist
Ronda Pattison—Colorist
Wilson Ramos Jr.—Letterer

"UNDER REMOTE CONTROL"
Andrew Brooks—Writer
Angela Zhang—Artist
Ronda Pattison—Colorist
Wilson Ramos Jr.—Letterer

"GAME OVER"
Derek Fridolfs—Writer
Gizelle Orbino—Artist, Colorist
Wilson Ramos Jr.—Letterer

"FLIPPING THE SCRIPT"
Andrew Brooks—Writer
Gizelle Orbino—Artist, Colorist
Wilson Ramos Jr.—Letterer

"I'M WITH THE BAND"
Angela Entzminger—Writer
Lee-Roy Lahey—Penciler
Zazo Aguiar—Inker, Colorist
Wilson Ramos Jr.—Letterer

"FACE VALUE"
Andrew Brooks—Writer, Artist, Colorist
Wilson Ramos Jr.—Letterer

"IMPROMPTOOT CONCERT"
Derek Fridolfs —Writer
Melissa Kleynowski—Penciler
Zazo Aguiar—Inker, Colorist
Wilson Ramos Jr.—Letterer

"CRUMBINAL JUSTICE"
Andrew Brooks—Writer
Erin Hyde—Artist, Colorist
Wilson Ramos Jr.—Letterer

"LOW ACHIEVEMENT"
Derek Fridolfs—Writer
Gizelle Orbino—Artist, Colorist, Letterer

"THE LOUD HOUSE GAMES!"
Brian Smith—Writer, Artist, Colorist
Wilson Ramos Jr.—Letterer

"FIND OF THE CENTURY"
Angela Entzminger—Writer
Colton Davis—Artist
Gabrielle Dolbey—Colorist
Wilson Ramos Jr.—Letterer

"A MONSTER PLAN"
Derek Fridolfs—Writer
Angela Zhang—Artist
Ronda Pattison—Colorist
Wilson Ramos Jr.—Letterer

"OUT OF TUNE"
Andrew Brooks—Writer
Daniela Rodriguez—Artist
Erin Hyde—Colorist
Wilson Ramos Jr.—Letterer

"DEUCES WILD!"
Chris Savino, Karla Sakas Shropshire—Writers
Miguel Puga, Jared Morgan, Chris Savino, Jordan Rosato—Artists, Letterers
Amanda Rynda—Colorist

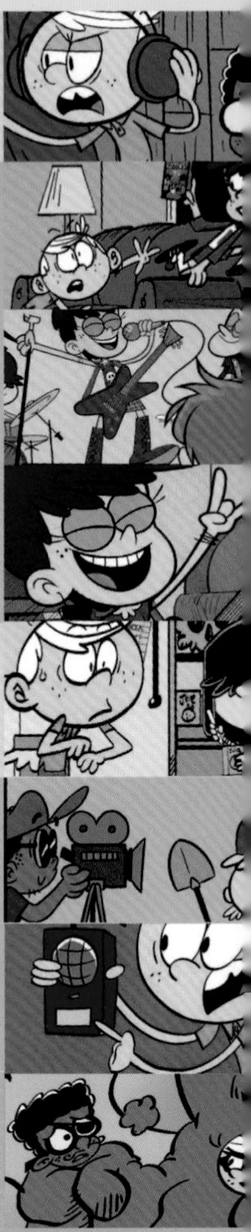

Cover by THE LOUD HOUSE DESIGN TEAM
JAMES SALERNO —Sr. Art Director/Nickelodeon
JAYJAY JACKSON—Design
ASHLEY KLIMENT, SEAN GANTKA, ANGELA ENTZMINGER, DANA CLUVERIUS, MOLLIE FREILICH, AMANDA RYNDA—Special Thanks
JEFF WHITMAN—Editor
KARR ANTUNES—Editorial Intern
JOAN HILTY — Comics Editor/Nickelodeon
JIM SALICRUP
Editor-in-Chief

ISBN: 978-1-6299-1797-9 paperback edition
ISBN: 978-1-6299-1796-2 hardcover edition

www.papercutz.com

Papercutz books may be purchased for business or promotional use. For information on bulk purchases please contact Macmillan Corporate and Premium Sales Department at (800) 221-7945 x5442.

Printed in China
August 2019

Distributed by Macmillan
First Printing

MEET THE LOUD FAMILY *and friends!*

LINCOLN LOUD
THE MIDDLE CHILD (11)

At 11 years old, Lincoln is the middle child, with five older sisters and five younger sisters. He has learned that surviving the Loud household means staying a step ahead. He's the man with a plan, always coming up with a way to get what he wants or deal with a problem, even if things inevitably go wrong. Being the only boy comes with some perks. Lincoln gets his own room – even if it's just a converted linen closet. On the other hand, being the only boy also means he sometimes gets a little too much attention from his sisters. They mother him, tease him, and use him as the occasional lab rat or fashion show participant. Lincoln's sisters may drive him crazy, but he loves them and is always willing to help out if they need him.

LORI LOUD
THE OLDEST (17)

As the first-born child of the Loud Clan, Lori sees herself as the boss of all her siblings. She feels she's paved the way for them and deserves extra respect. Her signature traits are rolling her eyes, texting her boyfriend, Bobby, and literally saying "literally" all the time. Because she's the oldest and most experienced sibling, Lori can be a great ally, so it pays to stay on her good side, especially since she can drive.

LENI LOUD
THE FASHIONISTA (16)

Leni spends most of her time designing outfits and accessorizing. She always falls for Luan's pranks, and sometimes walks into walls when she's talking (she's not great at doing two things at once). Leni might be flighty, but she's the sweetest of the Loud siblings and truly has a heart of gold (even though she's pretty sure it's a heart of blood).

LUNA LOUD
THE ROCK STAR (15)

Luna is loud, boisterous and freewheeling, and her energy is always cranked to 11. She thinks about music so much that she even talks in song lyrics. On the off-chance she doesn't have her guitar with her, everything can and will be turned into a musical instrument. You can always count on Luna to help out, and she'll do most anything you ask, as long as you're okay with her supplying a rocking guitar accompaniment.

LUAN LOUD
THE JOKESTER (14)

Luan's a standup comedienne who provides a nonstop barrage of silly puns. She's big on prop comedy too – squirting flowers and whoopee cushions – so you have to be on your toes whenever she's around. She loves to pull pranks and is a really good ventriloquist – she is often found doing bits with her dummy, Mr. Coconuts. Luan never lets anything get her down; to her, laughter IS the best medicine.

EL DIABLO

HOPS

LYNN LOUD
THE ATHLETE (13)

Lynn is athletic and full of energy and is always looking for a teammate. With her, it's all sports all the time. She'll turn anything into a sport. Putting away eggs? Jump shot! Score! Cleaning up the eggs? Slap shot! Score! Lynn is very competitive, but despite her competitive nature, she always tries to just have a good time.

LUCY LOUD
THE EMO (8)

You can always count on Lucy to give the morbid point of view in any given situation. She is obsessed with all things spooky and dark – funerals, vampires, séances, and the like. She wears mostly black and writes moody poetry. She's usually quiet and keeps to herself. Lucy has a way of mysteriously appearing out of nowhere, and try as they might, her siblings never get used to this.

LOLA LOUD
THE BEAUTY QUEEN (6)

Lola could not be more different from her twin sister, Lana. She's a pageant powerhouse whose interests include glitter, photo shoots, and her own beautiful, beautiful face. But don't let her cute, gap-toothed smile fool you; underneath all the sugar and spice lurks a Machiavellian mastermind. Whatever Lola wants, Lola gets – or else. She's the eyes and ears of the household and never resists an opportunity to tattle on troublemakers. But if you stay on Lola's good side, you've got yourself a fierce ally – and a lifetime supply of free makeovers.

LANA LOUD
THE TOMBOY (6)

Lana is the rough-and-tumble sparkplug counterpart to her twin sister, Lola. She's all about reptiles, mud pies, and muffler repair. She's the resident Ms. Fix-it and is always ready to lend a hand – the dirtier the job, the better. Need your toilet unclogged? Snake fed? Back-zit popped? Lana's your gal. All she asks in return is a little A-B-C gum, or a handful of kibble (she often sneaks it from the dog bowl).

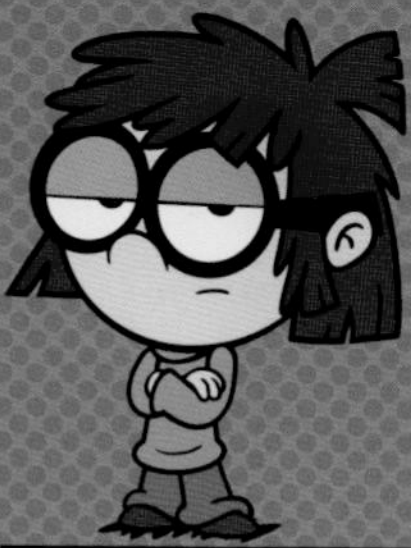

LISA LOUD
THE GENIUS (4)

Lisa is smarter than the rest of her siblings combined. She'll most likely be a rocket scientist, or a brain surgeon, or an evil genius who takes over the world. Lisa spends most of her time working in her lab (the family has gotten used to the explosions), and says her research leaves little time for frivolous human pursuits like "playing" or "getting haircuts." That said, she's always there to help with a homework question, or to explain why the sky is blue, or to point out the structural flaws in someone's pillow fort. Lisa says it's the least she can do for her favorite test subjects, er, siblings.

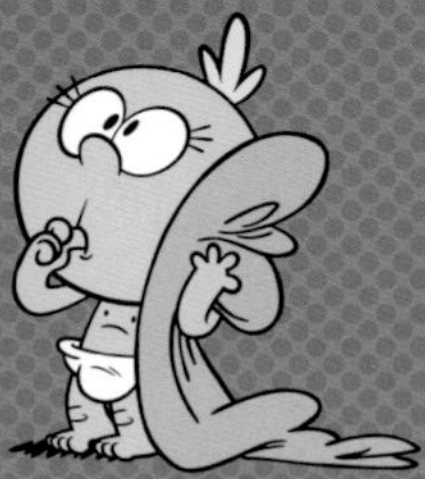

LILY LOUD
THE BABY (15 MONTHS)

Lily is a giggly, drooly, diaper-ditching free spirit, affectionately known as "the poop machine." You can't keep a nappy on this kid – she's like a teething Houdini. But even when Lily's running wild, dropping rancid diaper bombs, or drooling all over the remote, she always brings a smile to everyone's face (and a clothespin to their nose). Lily is everyone's favorite little buddy, and the whole family loves her unconditionally.

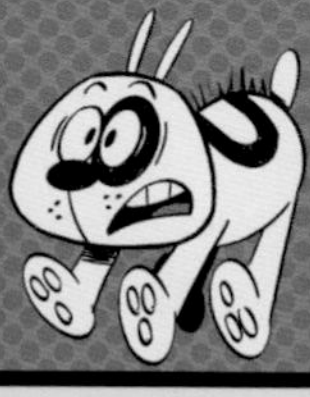

CHARLES

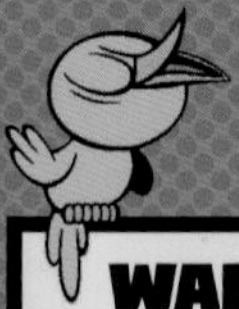

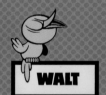

WALT

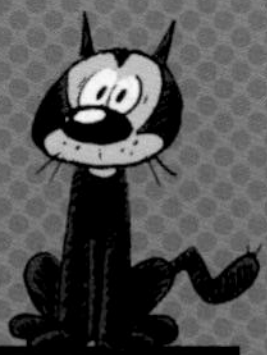

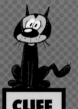

CLIFF

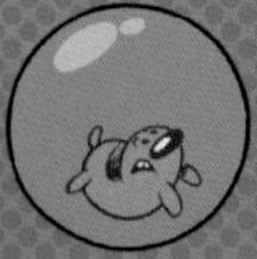

GEO

RITA LOUD

Mother to the eleven Loud kids, Mom (Rita Loud) wears many different hats. She's a chauffeur, homework-checker and barf-cleaner-upper all rolled into one. She's always there for her kids and ready to jump into action during a crisis, whether it's a fight between the twins or Leni's missing shoe. When she's not chasing the kids around or at her day job as a dental hygienist, Mom pursues her passion: writing. She also loves taking on house projects and is very handy with tools (guess that's where Lana gets it from). Between writing, working and being a mom, her days are always hectic but she wouldn't have it any other way.

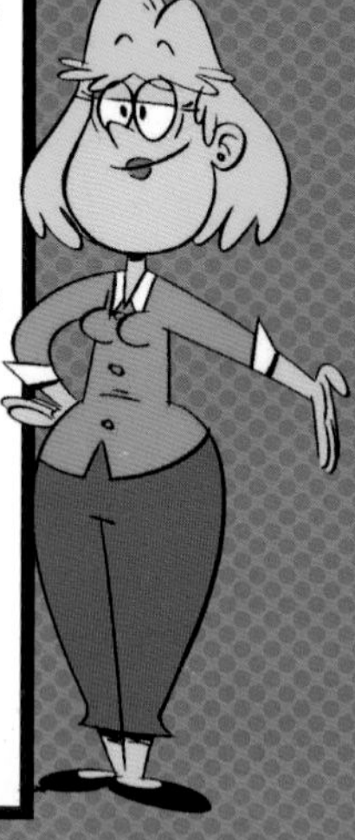

LYNN LOUD SR.

Dad (Lynn Loud Sr.) is a fun-loving, upbeat aspiring chef. A kid-at-heart, he's not above taking part in the kids' zany schemes. In addition to cooking, Dad loves his van, playing the cowbell and making puns. Before meeting Mom, Dad spent a semester in England and has been obsessed with British culture ever since – and sometimes "accidentally" slips into a British accent. When Dad's not wrangling the kids, he's pursuing his dream of opening his own restaurant where he hopes to make his "Lynn-sagnas" world-famous.

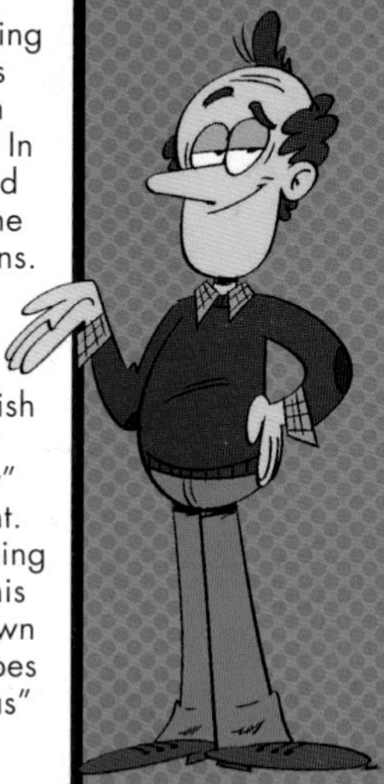

CLYDE McBRIDE
THE BEST FRIEND (11)

Clyde is Lincoln's partner in crime. He's always willing to go along with Lincoln's crazy schemes (even if he sees the flaws in them up-front). Lincoln and Clyde are two peas in a pod and share pretty much all of the same tastes in movies, comics, TV shows, toys—you name it. As an only child, Clyde envies Lincoln—how cool would it be to always have siblings around to talk to? But since Clyde spends so much time at the Loud household, he's almost an honorary sibling anyway.

ZACH GURDLE

Zach is a self-admitted nerd who's obsessed with aliens and conspiracy theories. He lives between a freeway and a circus, so the chaos of the Loud House doesn't faze him. He and Rusty occasionally butt heads, but deep down, it's all love.

RUSTY SPOKES

Rusty is a self-proclaimed ladies' man who's always the first to dish out girl advice— even though he's never been on an actual date. His dad owns a suit rental service, so occasionally Rusty can hook the gang up with some dapper duds—just as long as no one gets anything dirty.

LIAM

Liam is an enthusiastic, sweet-natured farm boy full of down-home wisdom. He loves hanging out with his Mee Maw, wrestling his prize pig Virginia, and sharing his farm-to-table produce with the rest of the gang.

VIRGINIA

STELLA

Stella, 11, is a quirky, carefree girl who's new to Royal Woods. She has tons of interests, like trying on wigs, playing laser tag, eating curly fries, and hanging with her friends. But what she loves the most is tech — she always wants to dismantle electronics and put them back together again.

SAM SHARP

SULLY

MAZZY

LUNA'S BANDMATES

"BUSINESS CENTS"

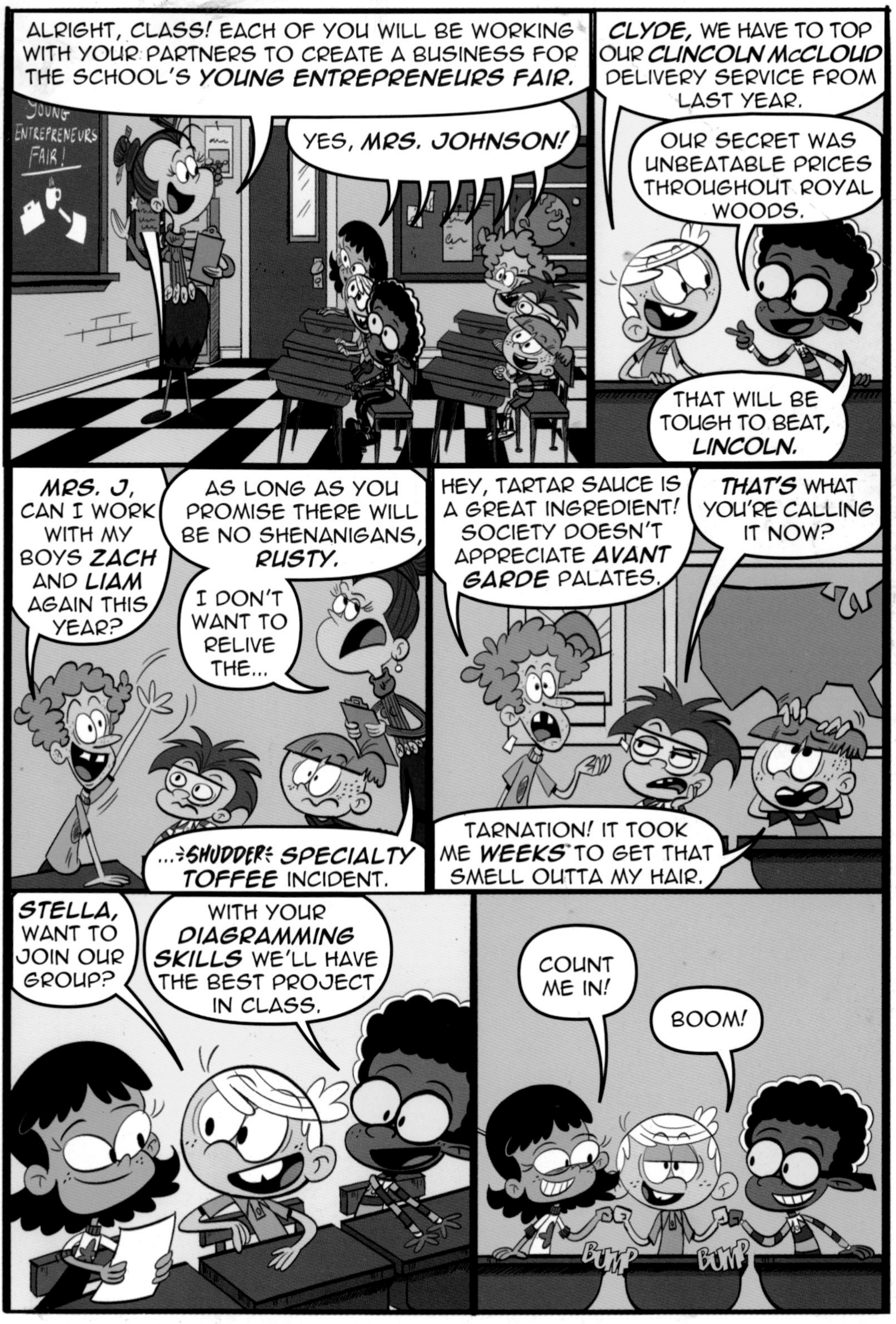
ALRIGHT, CLASS! EACH OF YOU WILL BE WORKING WITH YOUR PARTNERS TO CREATE A BUSINESS FOR THE SCHOOL'S YOUNG ENTREPRENEURS FAIR.
YOUNG ENTREPRENEURS FAIR!
YES, MRS. JOHNSON!
CLYDE, WE HAVE TO TOP OUR CLINCOLN McCLOUD DELIVERY SERVICE FROM LAST YEAR.
OUR SECRET WAS UNBEATABLE PRICES THROUGHOUT ROYAL WOODS.
THAT WILL BE TOUGH TO BEAT, LINCOLN.
MRS. J, CAN I WORK WITH MY BOYS ZACH AND LIAM AGAIN THIS YEAR?
AS LONG AS YOU PROMISE THERE WILL BE NO SHENANIGANS, RUSTY.
I DON'T WANT TO RELIVE THE...
...SHUDDER SPECIALTY TOFFEE INCIDENT.
HEY, TARTAR SAUCE IS A GREAT INGREDIENT! SOCIETY DOESN'T APPRECIATE AVANT GARDE PALATES.
THAT'S WHAT YOU'RE CALLING IT NOW?
TARNATION! IT TOOK ME WEEKS TO GET THAT SMELL OUTTA MY HAIR.
STELLA, WANT TO JOIN OUR GROUP?
WITH YOUR DIAGRAMMING SKILLS WE'LL HAVE THE BEST PROJECT IN CLASS.
COUNT ME IN!
BOOM!
BUMP
BUMP

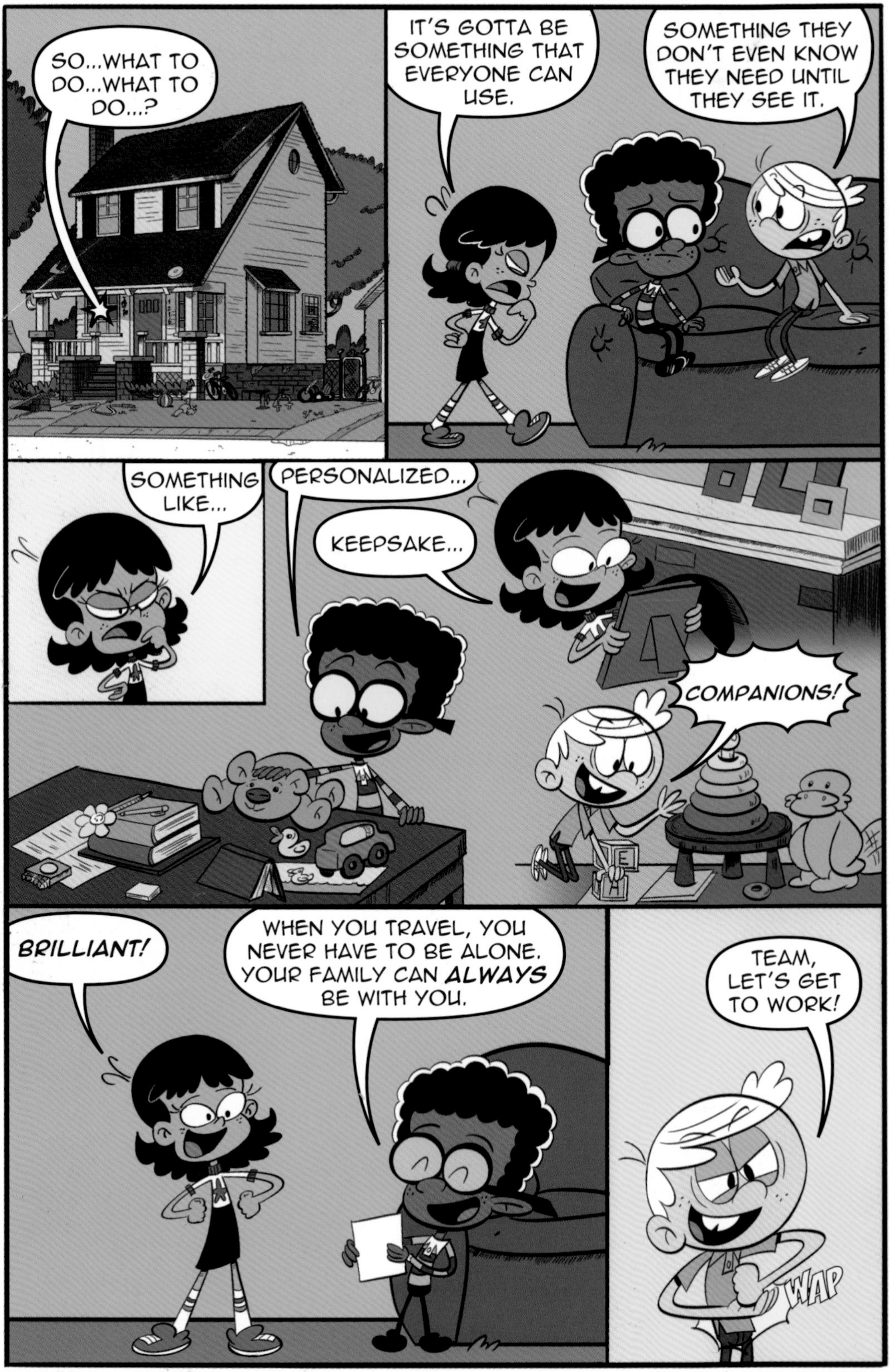
SO...WHAT TO DO...WHAT TO DO...?
IT'S GOTTA BE SOMETHING THAT EVERYONE CAN USE.
SOMETHING THEY DON'T EVEN KNOW THEY NEED UNTIL THEY SEE IT.
SOMETHING LIKE...
PERSONALIZED...
KEEPSAKE...
COMPANIONS!
BRILLIANT!
WHEN YOU TRAVEL, YOU NEVER HAVE TO BE ALONE. YOUR FAMILY CAN ALWAYS BE WITH YOU.
TEAM, LET'S GET TO WORK!
WAP

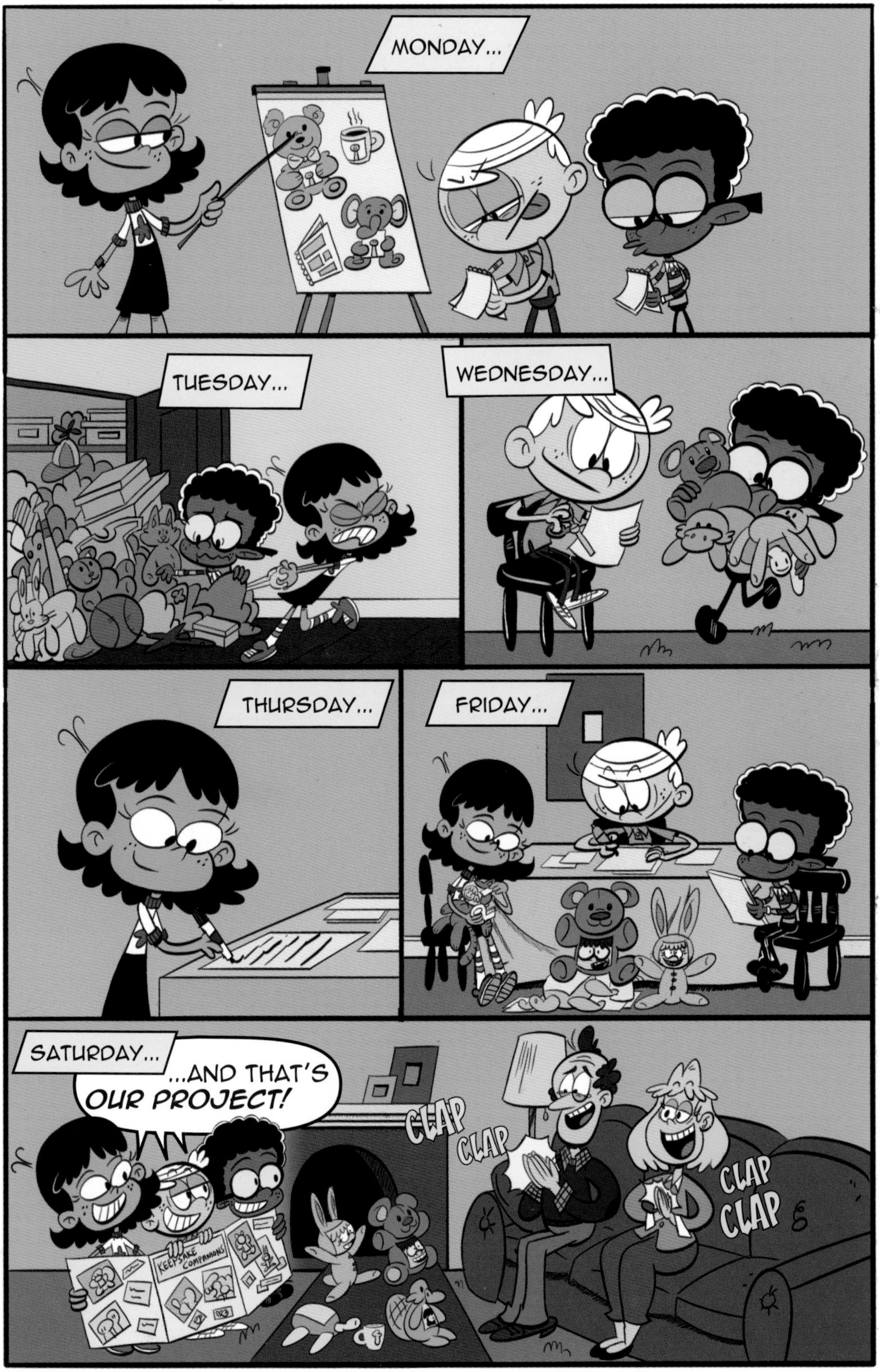
MONDAY...
TUESDAY...
WEDNESDAY...
THURSDAY...
FRIDAY...
SATURDAY...
...AND THAT'S OUR PROJECT!
KEEPSAKE COMPANIONS
CLAP
CLAP
CLAP
CLAP

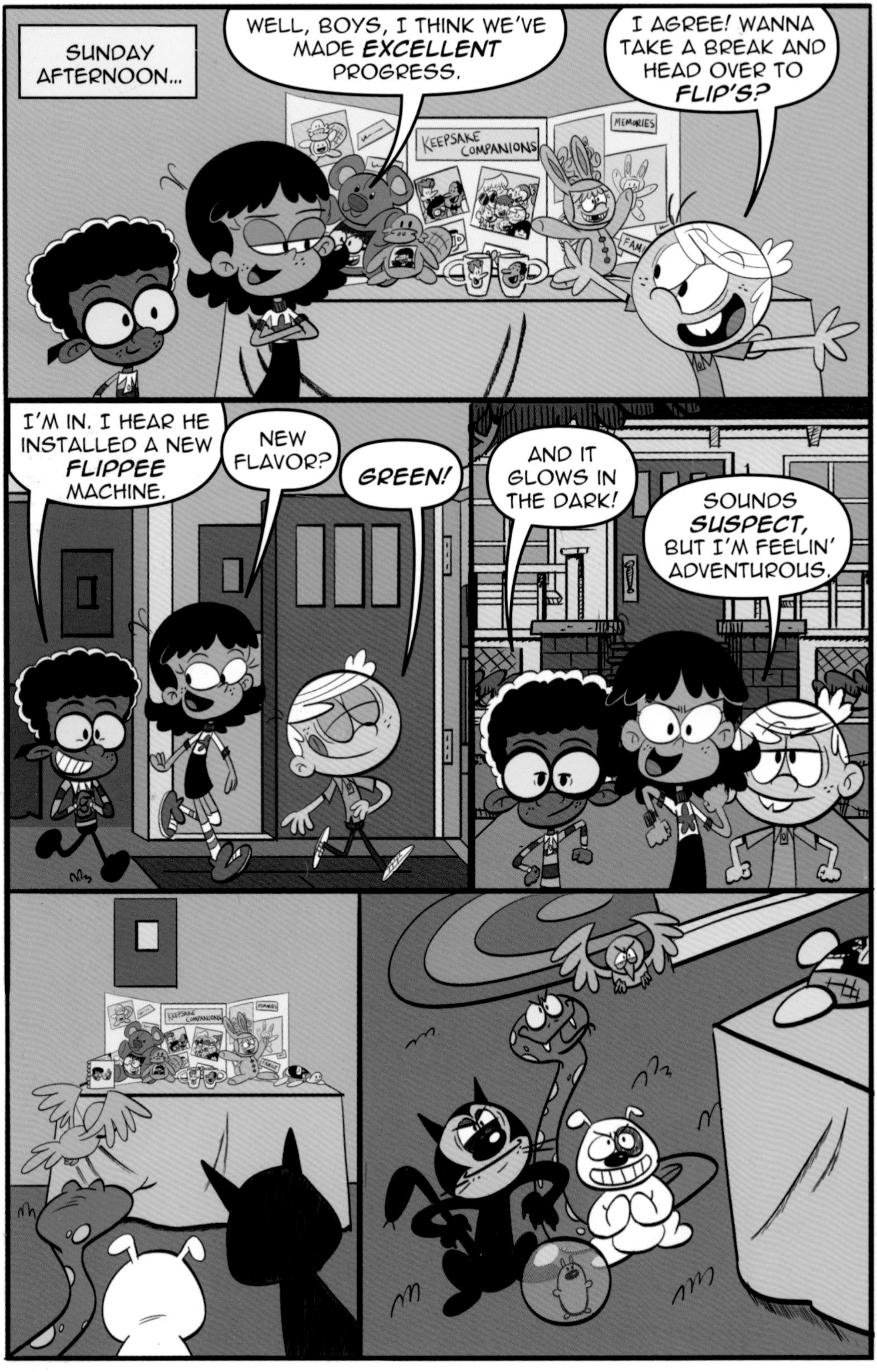
SUNDAY AFTERNOON...
WELL, BOYS, I THINK WE'VE MADE EXCELLENT PROGRESS.
I AGREE! WANNA TAKE A BREAK AND HEAD OVER TO FLIP'S?
KEEPSAKE COMPANIONS
MEMORIES
I'M IN. I HEAR HE INSTALLED A NEW FLIPPEE MACHINE.
NEW FLAVOR?
GREEN!
AND IT GLOWS IN THE DARK!
SOUNDS SUSPECT, BUT I'M FEELIN' ADVENTUROUS.
KEEPSAKE COMPANIONS
MEMORIES

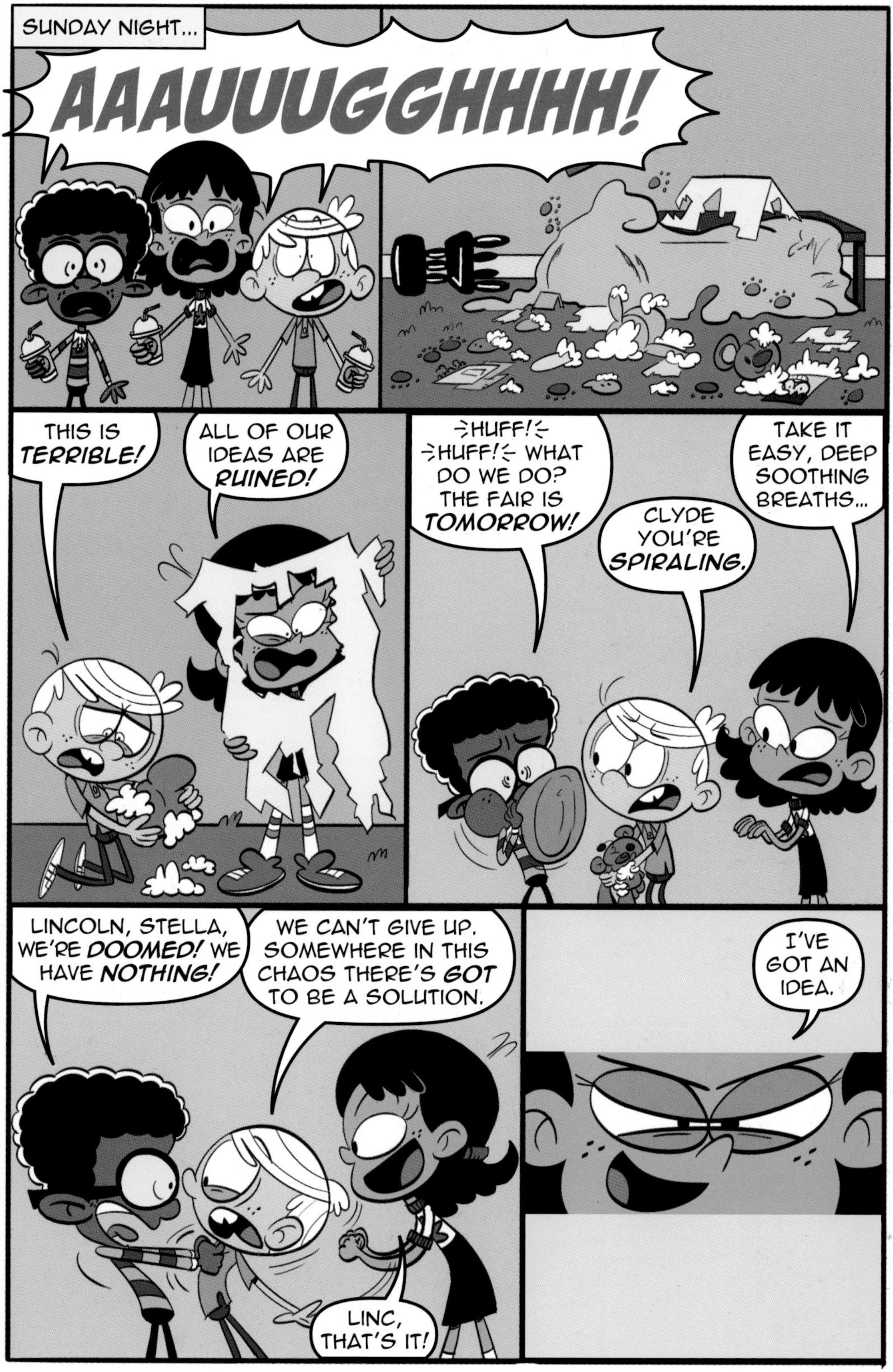
SUNDAY NIGHT...
AAAUUUGGHHHH!
THIS IS TERRIBLE!
ALL OF OUR IDEAS ARE RUINED!
HUFF! HUFF! WHAT DO WE DO? THE FAIR IS TOMORROW!
CLYDE YOU'RE SPIRALING.
TAKE IT EASY, DEEP SOOTHING BREATHS...
LINCOLN, STELLA, WE'RE DOOMED! WE HAVE NOTHING!
WE CAN'T GIVE UP. SOMEWHERE IN THIS CHAOS THERE'S GOT TO BE A SOLUTION.
LINC, THAT'S IT!
I'VE GOT AN IDEA.

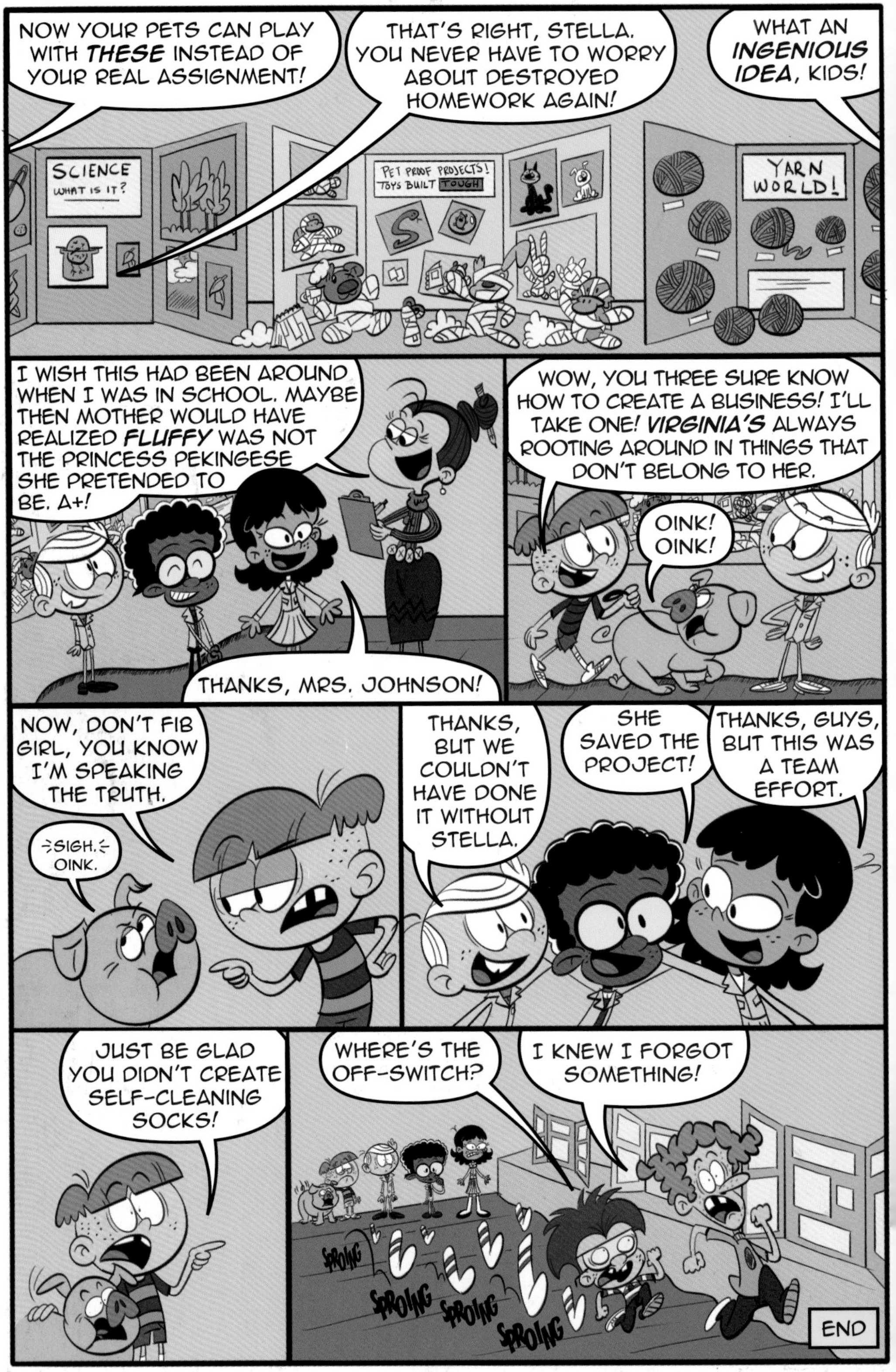

NOW YOUR PETS CAN PLAY WITH THESE INSTEAD OF YOUR REAL ASSIGNMENT!
THAT'S RIGHT, STELLA. YOU NEVER HAVE TO WORRY ABOUT DESTROYED HOMEWORK AGAIN!
WHAT AN INGENIOUS IDEA, KIDS!
SCIENCE WHAT IS IT?
PET PROOF PROJECTS! TOYS BUILT TOUGH
YARN WORLD!
I WISH THIS HAD BEEN AROUND WHEN I WAS IN SCHOOL. MAYBE THEN MOTHER WOULD HAVE REALIZED FLUFFY WAS NOT THE PRINCESS PEKINGESE SHE PRETENDED TO BE. A+!
THANKS, MRS. JOHNSON!
WOW, YOU THREE SURE KNOW HOW TO CREATE A BUSINESS! I'LL TAKE ONE! VIRGINIA'S ALWAYS ROOTING AROUND IN THINGS THAT DON'T BELONG TO HER.
OINK! OINK!
NOW, DON'T FIB GIRL, YOU KNOW I'M SPEAKING THE TRUTH.
SIGH. OINK.
THANKS, BUT WE COULDN'T HAVE DONE IT WITHOUT STELLA.
SHE SAVED THE PROJECT!
THANKS, GUYS, BUT THIS WAS A TEAM EFFORT.
JUST BE GLAD YOU DIDN'T CREATE SELF-CLEANING SOCKS!
WHERE'S THE OFF-SWITCH?
I KNEW I FORGOT SOMETHING!
SPROING
SPROING
SPROING
SPROING
END

"PREP TALK"

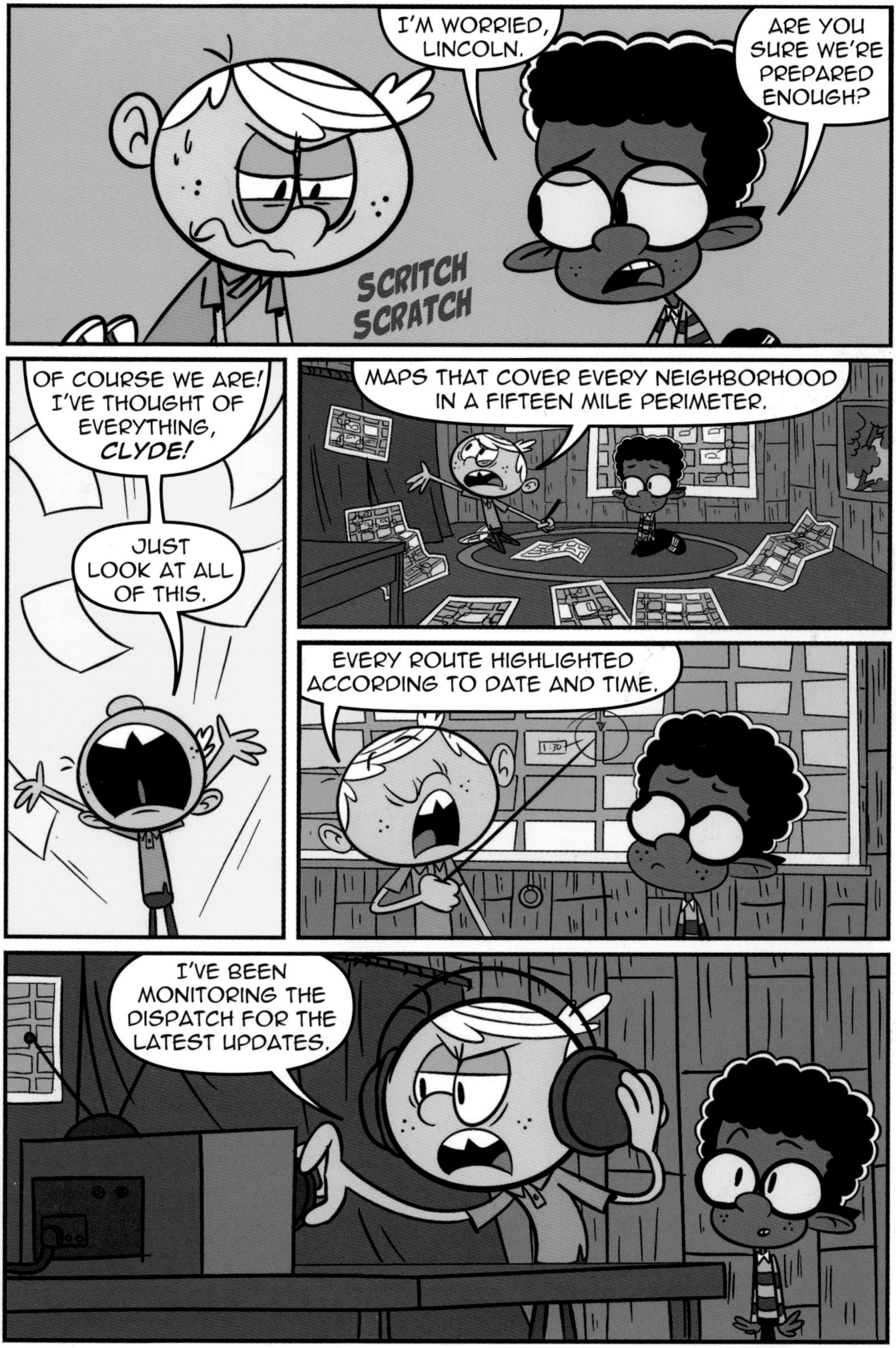
I'M WORRIED, LINCOLN.
ARE YOU SURE WE'RE PREPARED ENOUGH?
SCRITCH SCRATCH
OF COURSE WE ARE! I'VE THOUGHT OF EVERYTHING, *CLYDE!*
JUST LOOK AT ALL OF THIS.
MAPS THAT COVER EVERY NEIGHBORHOOD IN A FIFTEEN MILE PERIMETER.
EVERY ROUTE HIGHLIGHTED ACCORDING TO DATE AND TIME.
I'VE BEEN MONITORING THE DISPATCH FOR THE LATEST UPDATES.

WE HAVE THE LATEST IN SURVEILLANCE TECHNOLOGY, ON LOAN FROM *LISA.*

I'M LEAVING YOU IN CHARGE OF CENTRAL COMMAND AND I'LL BE YOUR EYES ON THE STREET.

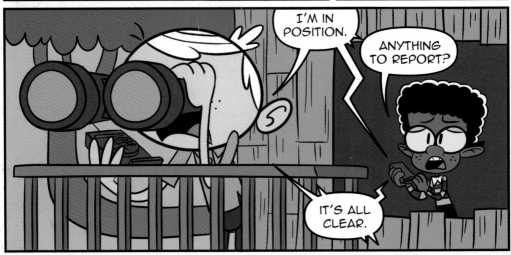

I'M IN POSITION.

ANYTHING TO REPORT?

IT'S ALL CLEAR.

AND NOW...*WE WAIT.*

TICK TICK TICK

WAIT FOR WHAT?

AHHH!

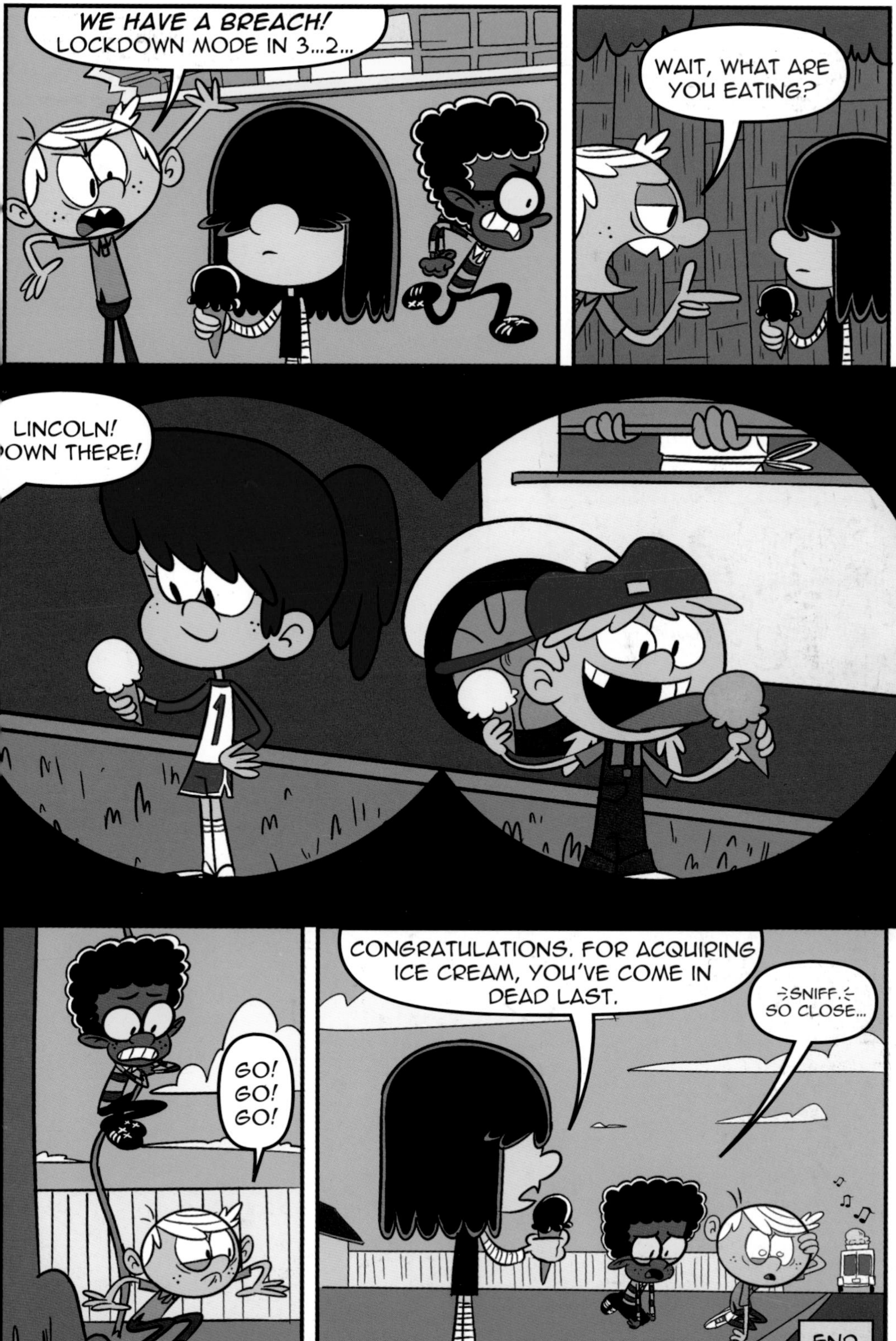
WE HAVE A BREACH! LOCKDOWN MODE IN 3...2...
WAIT, WHAT ARE YOU EATING?
LINCOLN! DOWN THERE!
GO! GO! GO!
CONGRATULATIONS. FOR ACQUIRING ICE CREAM, YOU'VE COME IN DEAD LAST.
SNIFF. SO CLOSE...
END

“UNDER REMOTE CONTROL”

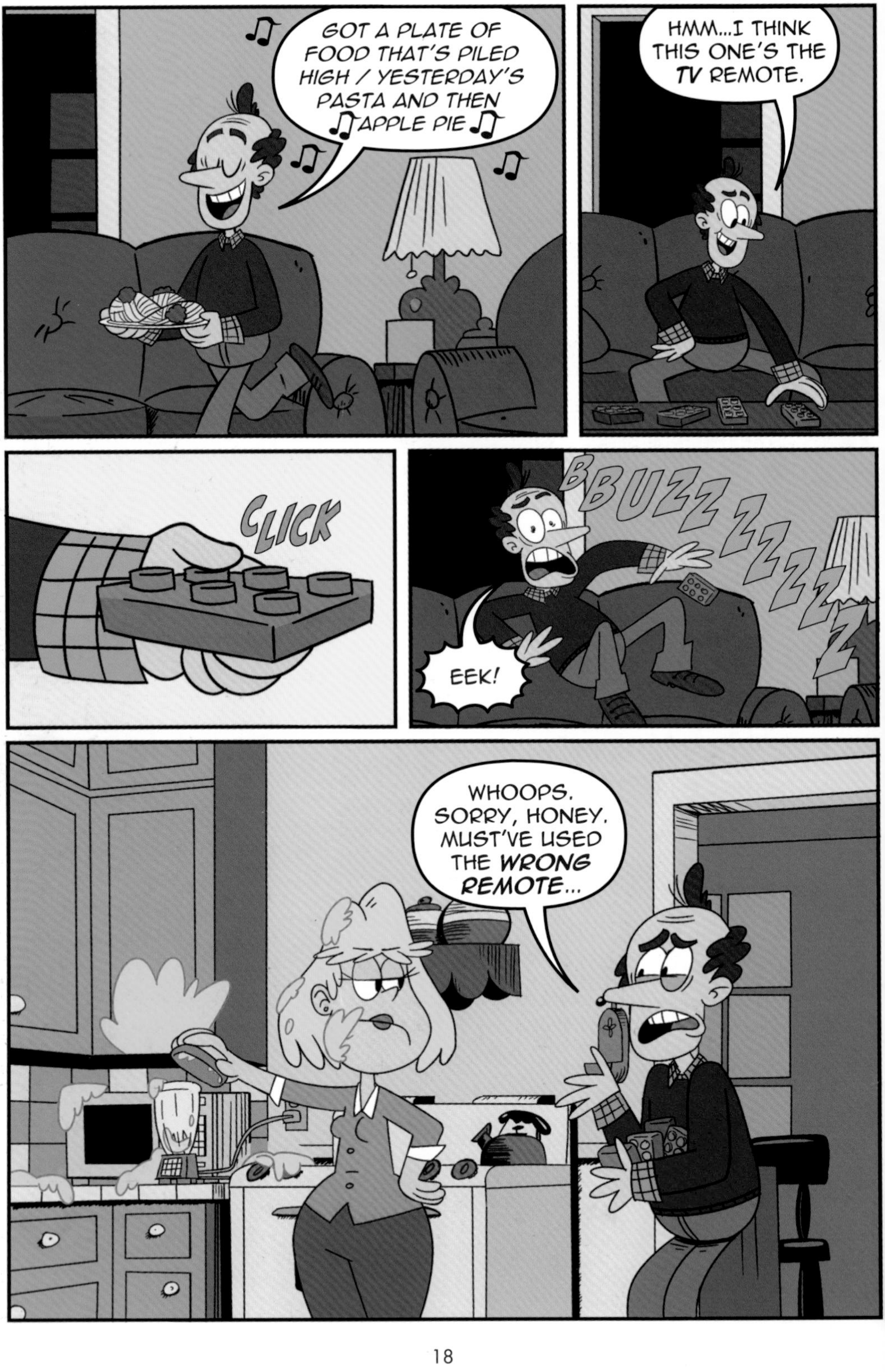
GOT A PLATE OF FOOD THAT'S PILED HIGH / YESTERDAY'S PASTA AND THEN ♫APPLE PIE♫
HMM...I THINK THIS ONE'S THE *TV* REMOTE.
CLICK
BBUZZZZZZZZZ
EEK!
WHOOPS. SORRY, HONEY. MUST'VE USED THE *WRONG REMOTE*...

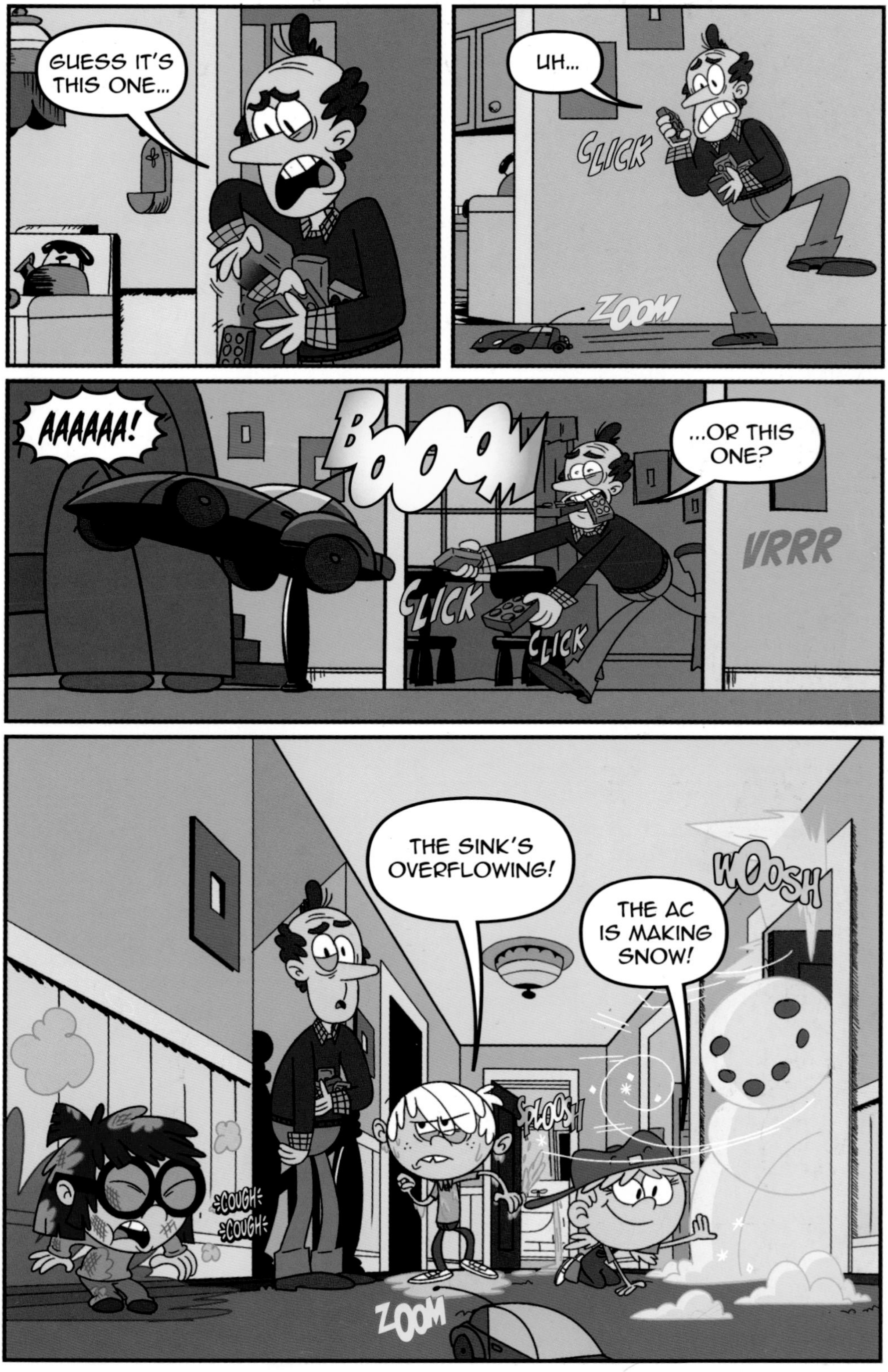
GUESS IT'S THIS ONE...
UH...
CLICK
ZOOM
AAAAAA!
BOOOM
...OR THIS ONE?
VRRR
CLICK
CLICK
THE SINK'S OVERFLOWING!
WOOSH
THE AC IS MAKING SNOW!
SPLOOSH
COUGH
COUGH
ZOOM

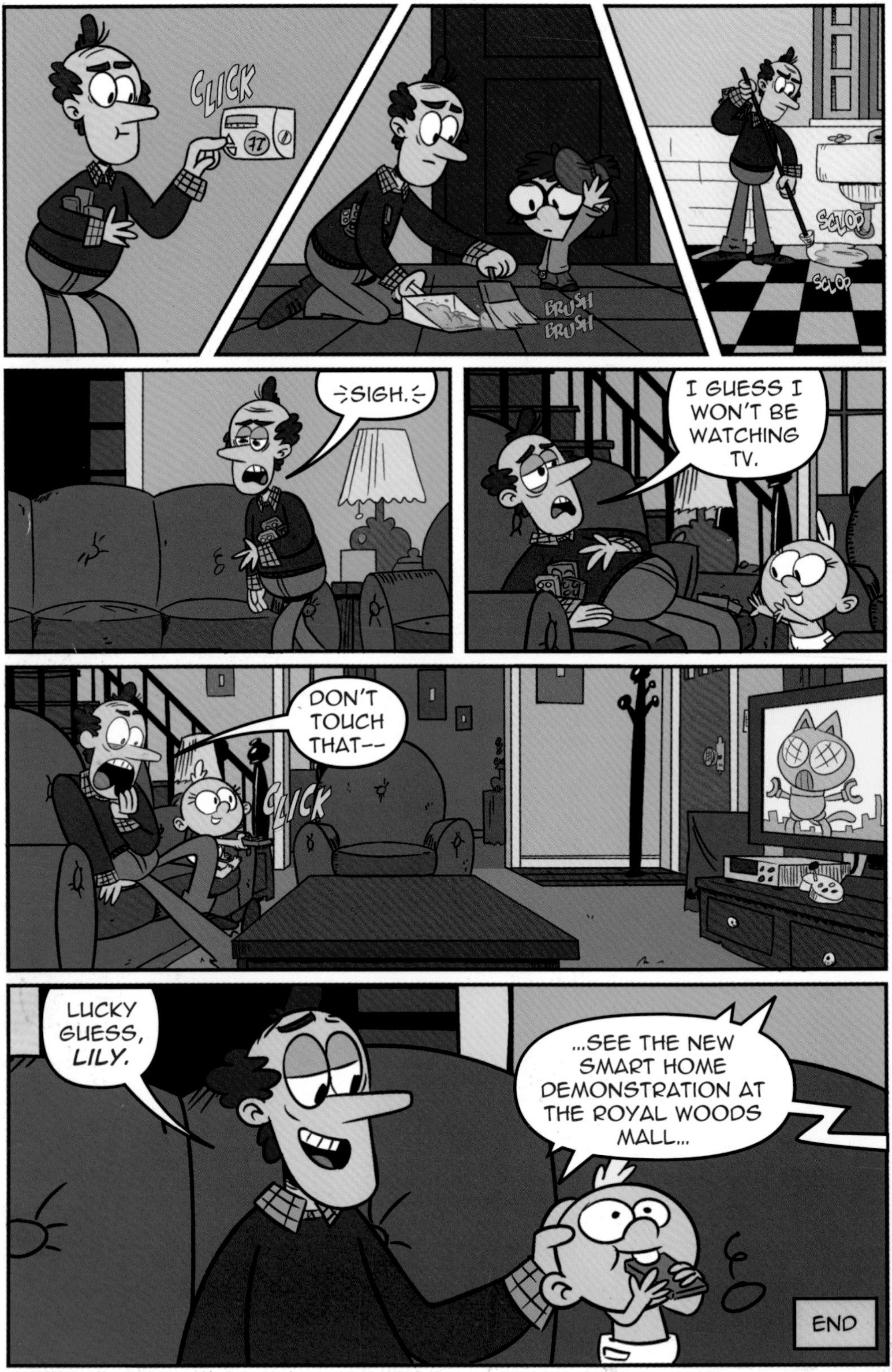
CLICK
BRUSH BRUSH
SCLOP
SCLOP
SIGH.
I GUESS I WON'T BE WATCHING TV.
DON'T TOUCH THAT--
CLICK
LUCKY GUESS, LILY.
...SEE THE NEW SMART HOME DEMONSTRATION AT THE ROYAL WOODS MALL...
END

"GAME OVER"

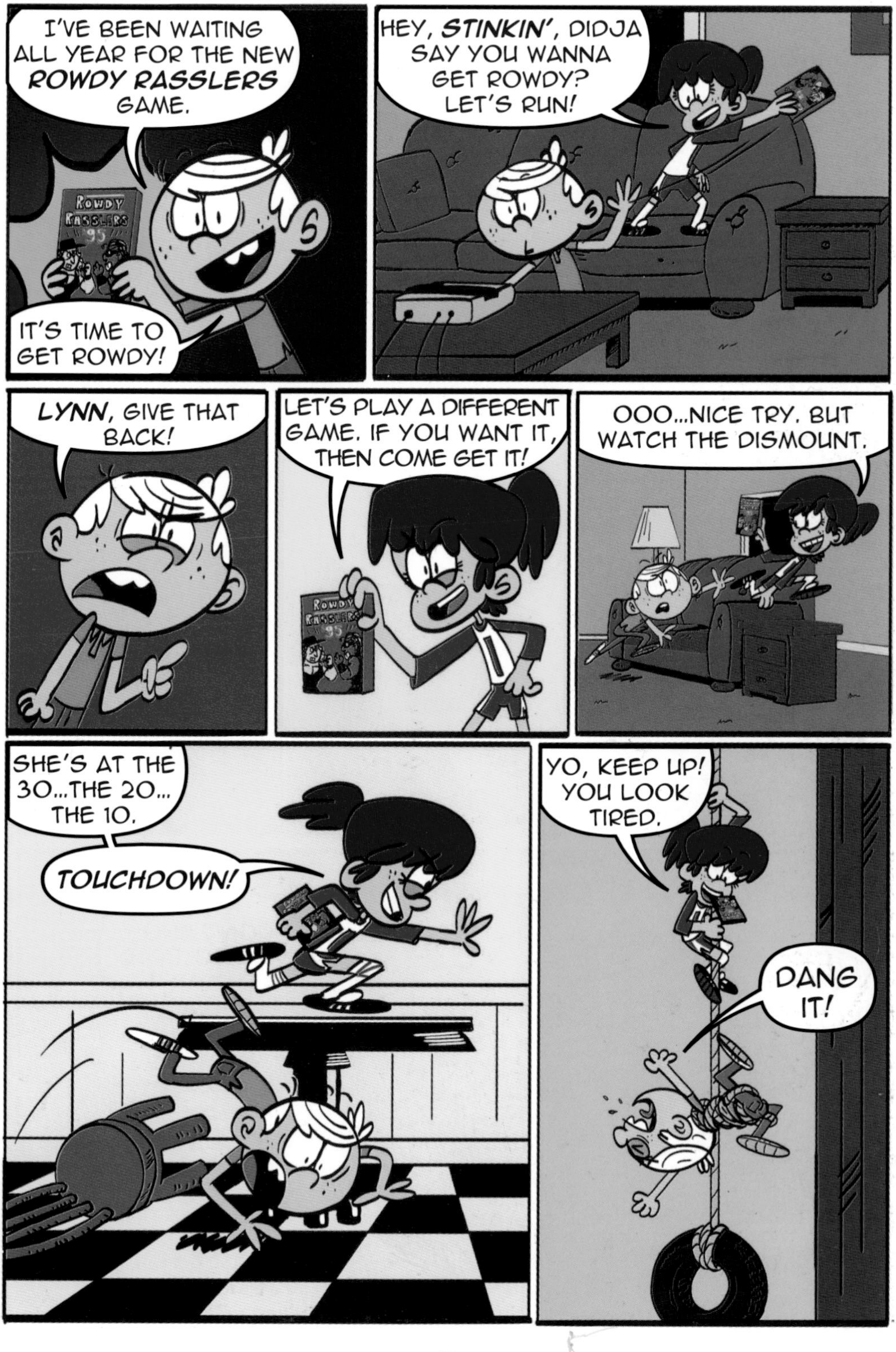

I'VE BEEN WAITING ALL YEAR FOR THE NEW *ROWDY RASSLERS* GAME.
IT'S TIME TO GET ROWDY!
ROWDY RASSLERS 95
HEY, *STINKIN'*, DIDJA SAY YOU WANNA GET ROWDY? LET'S RUN!
LYNN, GIVE THAT BACK!
LET'S PLAY A DIFFERENT GAME. IF YOU WANT IT, THEN COME GET IT!
ROWDY RASSLERS 95
OOO...NICE TRY. BUT WATCH THE DISMOUNT.
SHE'S AT THE 30...THE 20... THE 10.
TOUCHDOWN!
YO, KEEP UP! YOU LOOK TIRED.
DANG IT!

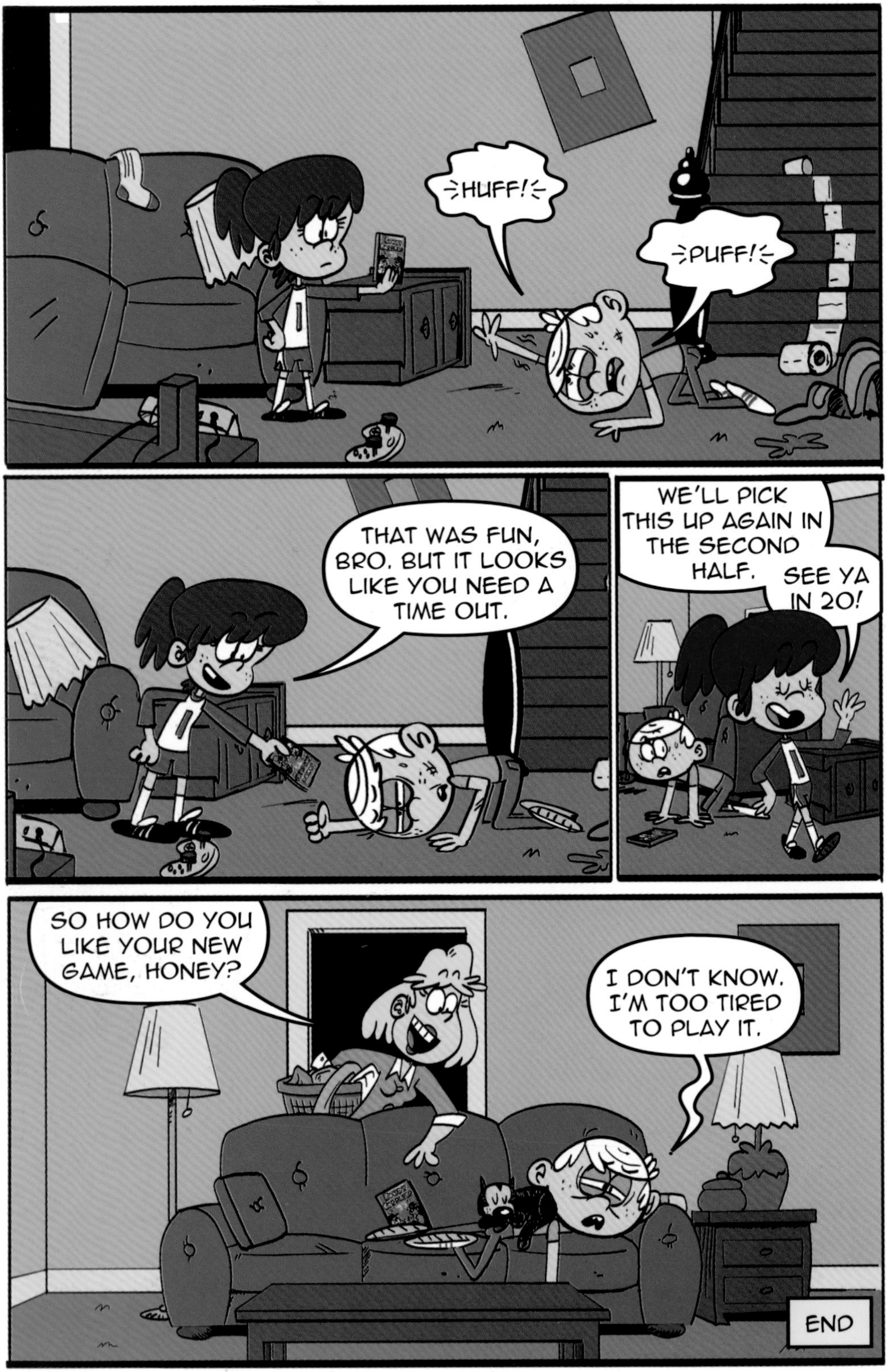

HUFF!
PUFF!
THAT WAS FUN, BRO. BUT IT LOOKS LIKE YOU NEED A TIME OUT.
WE'LL PICK THIS UP AGAIN IN THE SECOND HALF.
SEE YA IN 20!
SO HOW DO YOU LIKE YOUR NEW GAME, HONEY?
I DON'T KNOW. I'M TOO TIRED TO PLAY IT.
END

"FLIPPING THE SCRIPT"

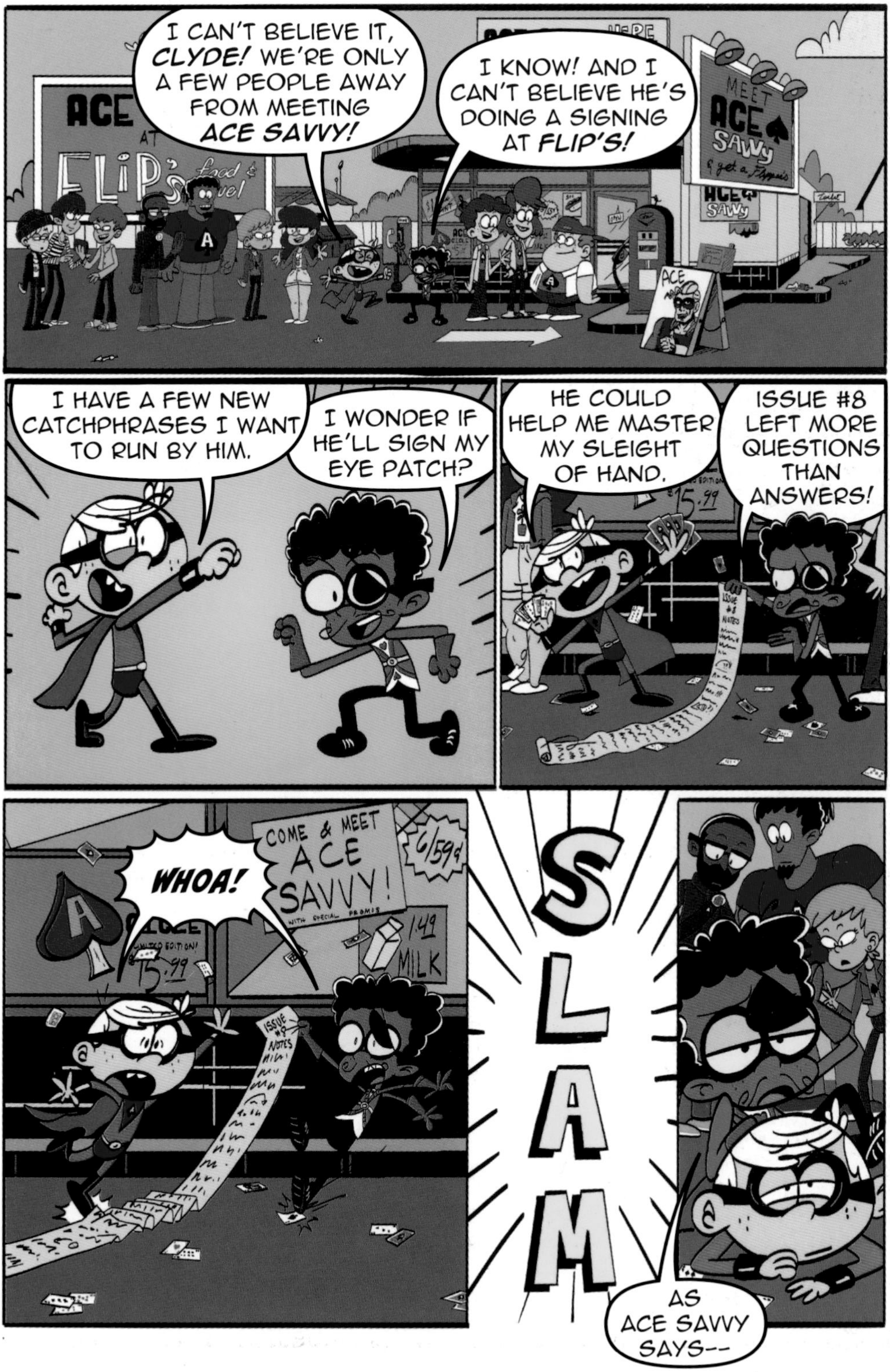

I CAN'T BELIEVE IT, *CLYDE!* WE'RE ONLY A FEW PEOPLE AWAY FROM MEETING *ACE SAVVY!*
I KNOW! AND I CAN'T BELIEVE HE'S DOING A SIGNING AT *FLIP'S!*
MEET ACE SAVVY
I HAVE A FEW NEW CATCHPHRASES I WANT TO RUN BY HIM.
I WONDER IF HE'LL SIGN MY EYE PATCH?
HE COULD HELP ME MASTER MY SLEIGHT OF HAND.
ISSUE #8 LEFT MORE QUESTIONS THAN ANSWERS!
COME & MEET ACE SAVVY!
WHOA!
1.49 MILK
SLAM
AS ACE SAVVY SAYS--

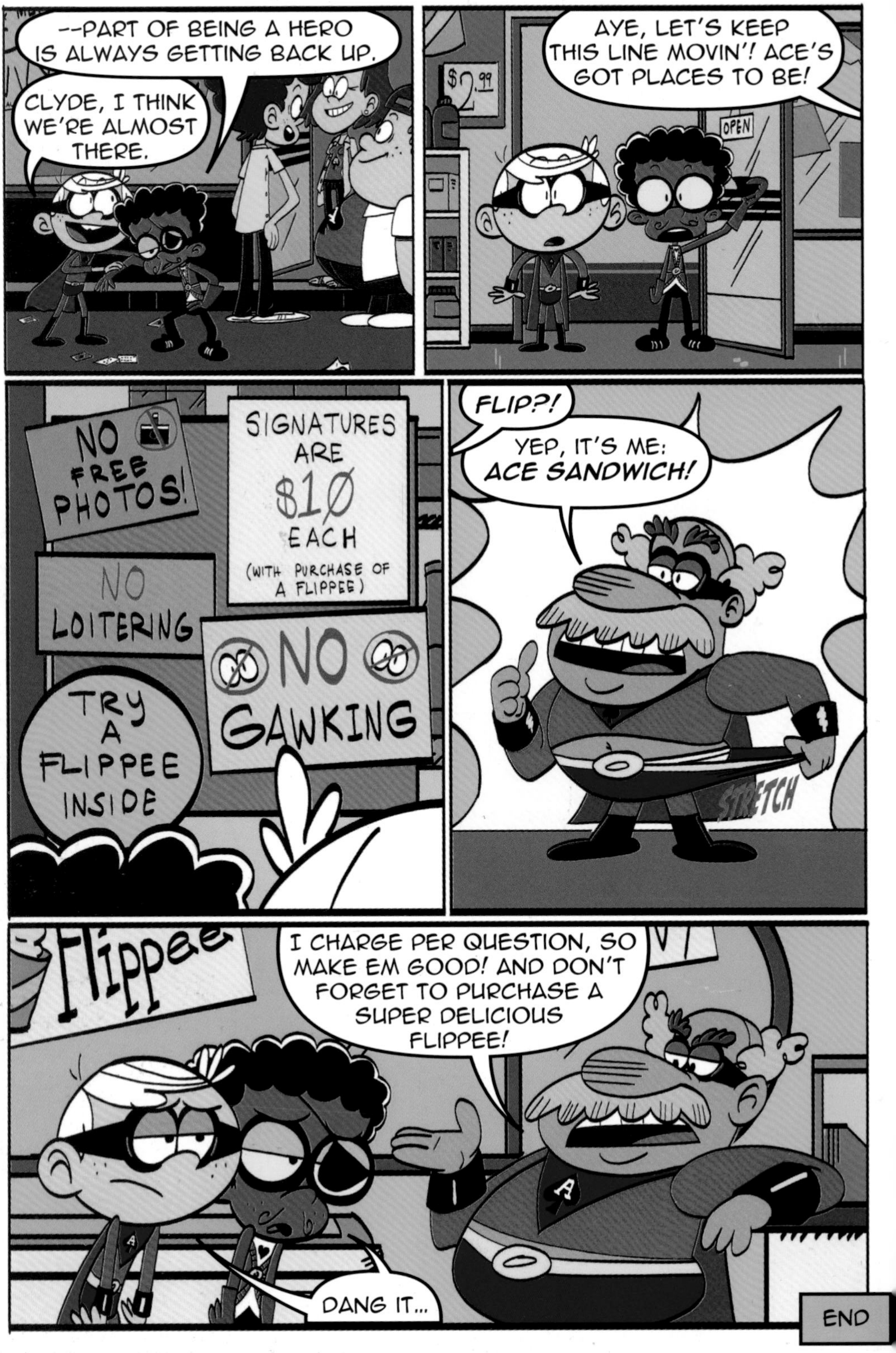
--PART OF BEING A HERO IS ALWAYS GETTING BACK UP.
CLYDE, I THINK WE'RE ALMOST THERE.
$2.99
AYE, LET'S KEEP THIS LINE MOVIN'! ACE'S GOT PLACES TO BE!
OPEN
NO FREE PHOTOS!
SIGNATURES ARE $10 EACH (WITH PURCHASE OF A FLIPPEE)
NO LOITERING
NO GAWKING
TRY A FLIPPEE INSIDE
FLIP?!
YEP, IT'S ME: ACE SANDWICH!
STRETCH
Flippee
I CHARGE PER QUESTION, SO MAKE EM GOOD! AND DON'T FORGET TO PURCHASE A SUPER DELICIOUS FLIPPEE!
DANG IT...
END

"I'M WITH THE BAND"

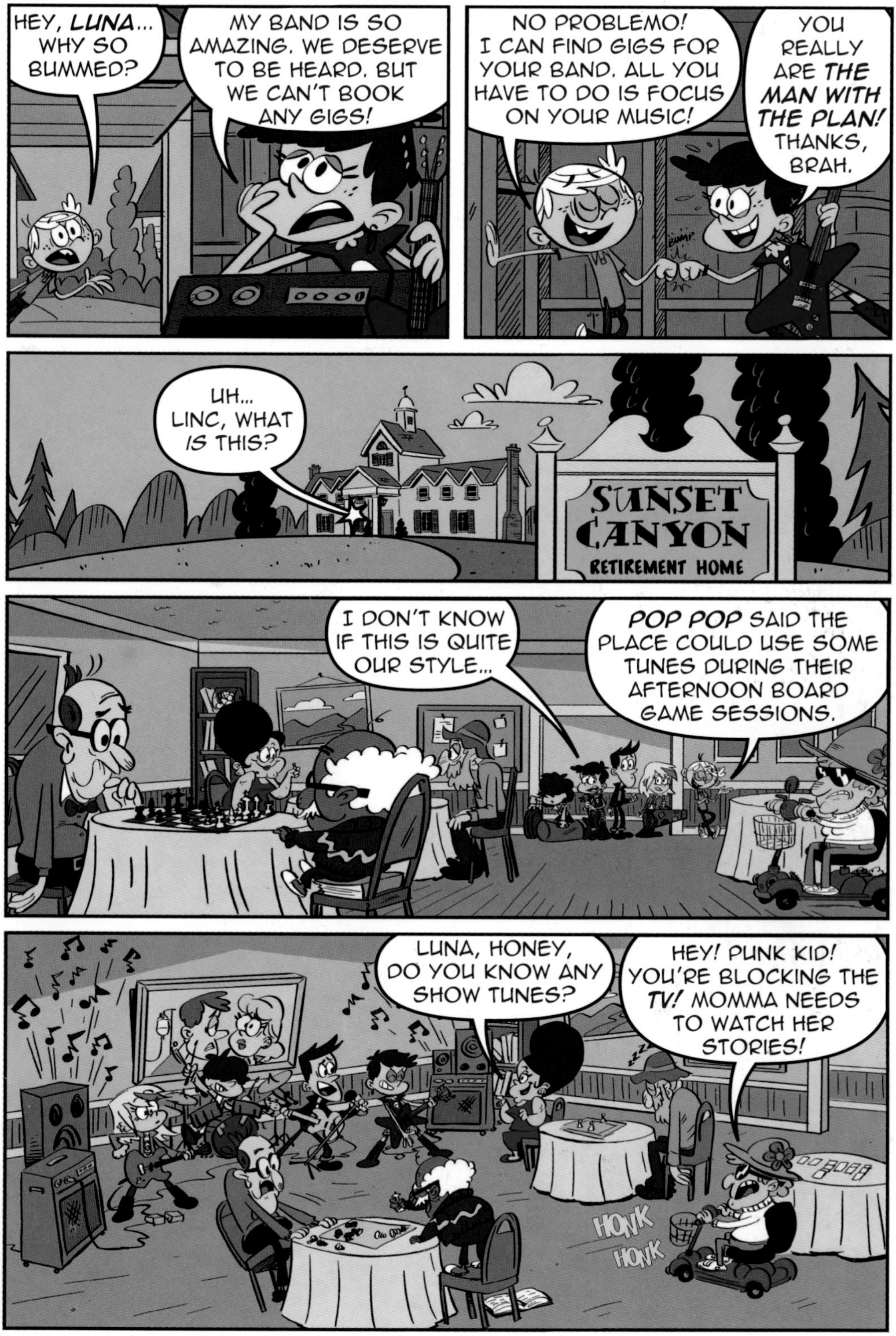
HEY, LUNA... WHY SO BUMMED?
MY BAND IS SO AMAZING. WE DESERVE TO BE HEARD. BUT WE CAN'T BOOK ANY GIGS!
NO PROBLEMO! I CAN FIND GIGS FOR YOUR BAND. ALL YOU HAVE TO DO IS FOCUS ON YOUR MUSIC!
YOU REALLY ARE THE MAN WITH THE PLAN! THANKS, BRAH.
BUMP
UH... LINC, WHAT IS THIS?
SUNSET CANYON
RETIREMENT HOME
I DON'T KNOW IF THIS IS QUITE OUR STYLE...
POP POP SAID THE PLACE COULD USE SOME TUNES DURING THEIR AFTERNOON BOARD GAME SESSIONS.
LUNA, HONEY, DO YOU KNOW ANY SHOW TUNES?
HEY! PUNK KID! YOU'RE BLOCKING THE TV! MOMMA NEEDS TO WATCH HER STORIES!
HONK
HONK

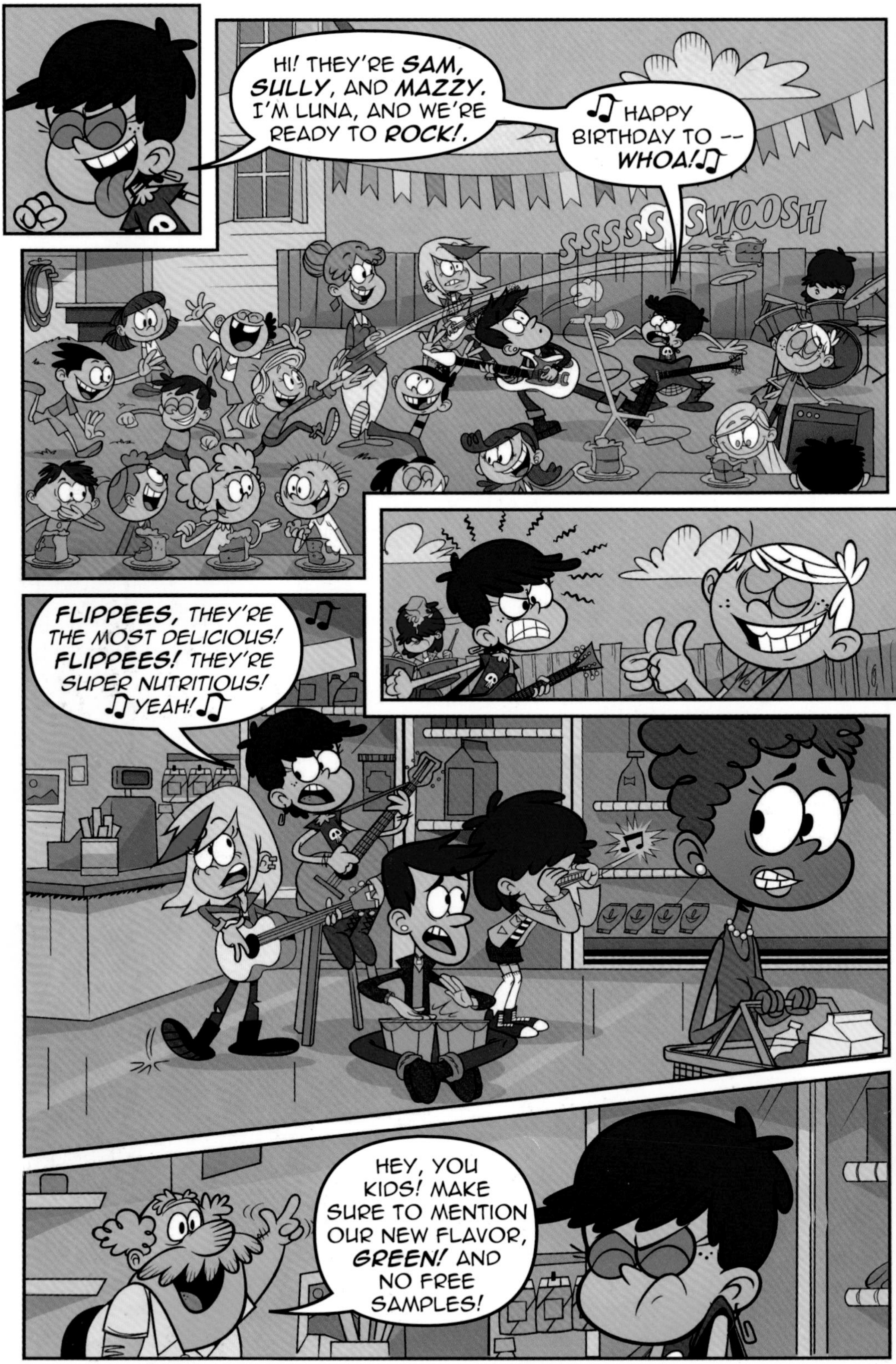

HI! THEY'RE SAM, SULLY, AND MAZZY. I'M LUNA, AND WE'RE READY TO ROCK!.
♫ HAPPY BIRTHDAY TO -- WHOA! ♫
SSSSSSWOOSH
FLIPPEES, THEY'RE THE MOST DELICIOUS! FLIPPEES! THEY'RE SUPER NUTRITIOUS! ♫ YEAH! ♫
HEY, YOU KIDS! MAKE SURE TO MENTION OUR NEW FLAVOR, GREEN! AND NO FREE SAMPLES!

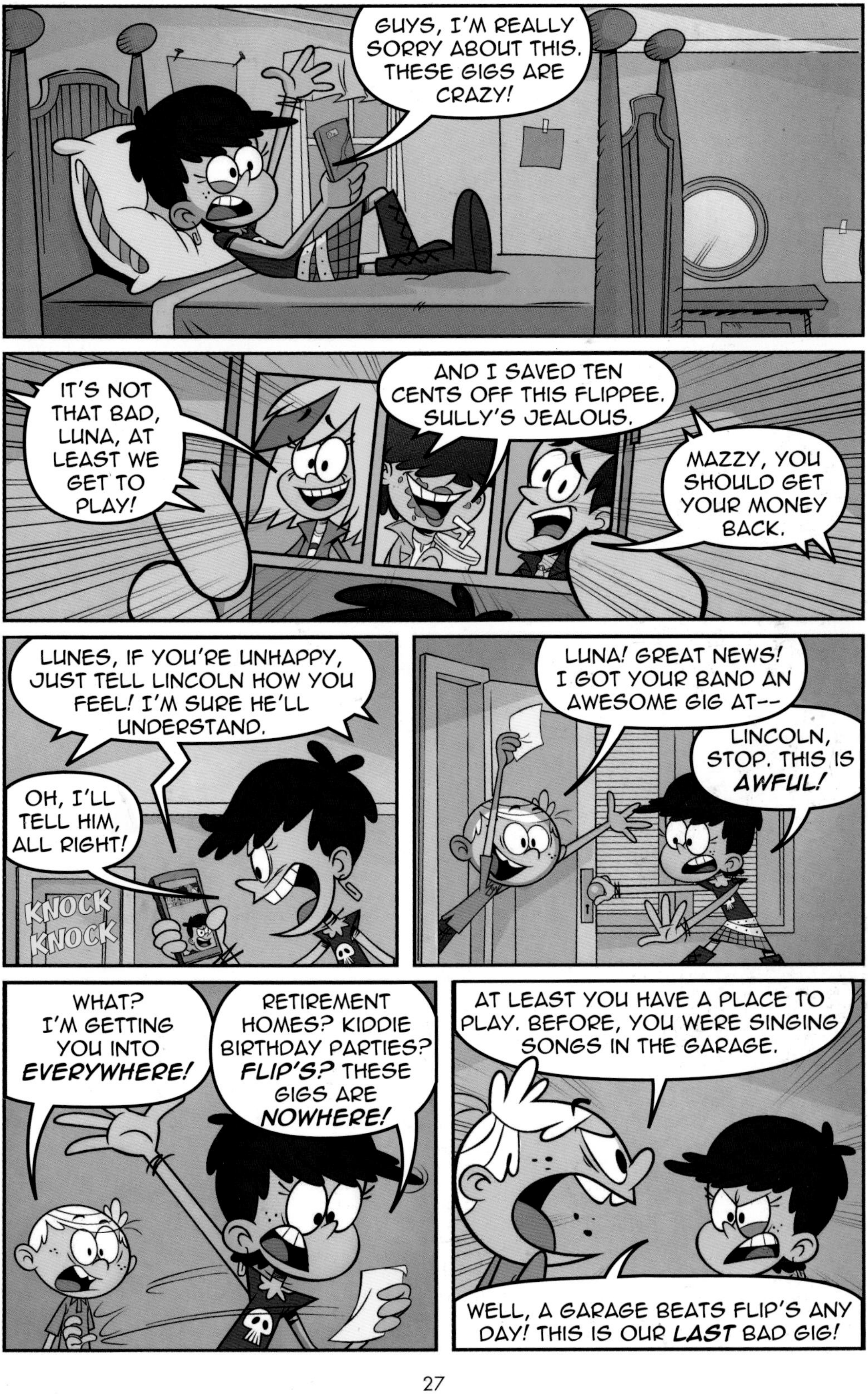
GUYS, I'M REALLY SORRY ABOUT THIS. THESE GIGS ARE CRAZY!
IT'S NOT THAT BAD, LUNA, AT LEAST WE GET TO PLAY!
AND I SAVED TEN CENTS OFF THIS FLIPPEE. SULLY'S JEALOUS.
MAZZY, YOU SHOULD GET YOUR MONEY BACK.
LUNES, IF YOU'RE UNHAPPY, JUST TELL LINCOLN HOW YOU FEEL! I'M SURE HE'LL UNDERSTAND.
OH, I'LL TELL HIM, ALL RIGHT!
KNOCK KNOCK
LUNA! GREAT NEWS! I GOT YOUR BAND AN AWESOME GIG AT--
LINCOLN, STOP. THIS IS *AWFUL!*
WHAT? I'M GETTING YOU INTO *EVERYWHERE!*
RETIREMENT HOMES? KIDDIE BIRTHDAY PARTIES? *FLIP'S?* THESE GIGS ARE *NOWHERE!*
AT LEAST YOU HAVE A PLACE TO PLAY. BEFORE, YOU WERE SINGING SONGS IN THE GARAGE.
WELL, A GARAGE BEATS FLIP'S ANY DAY! THIS IS OUR *LAST* BAD GIG!

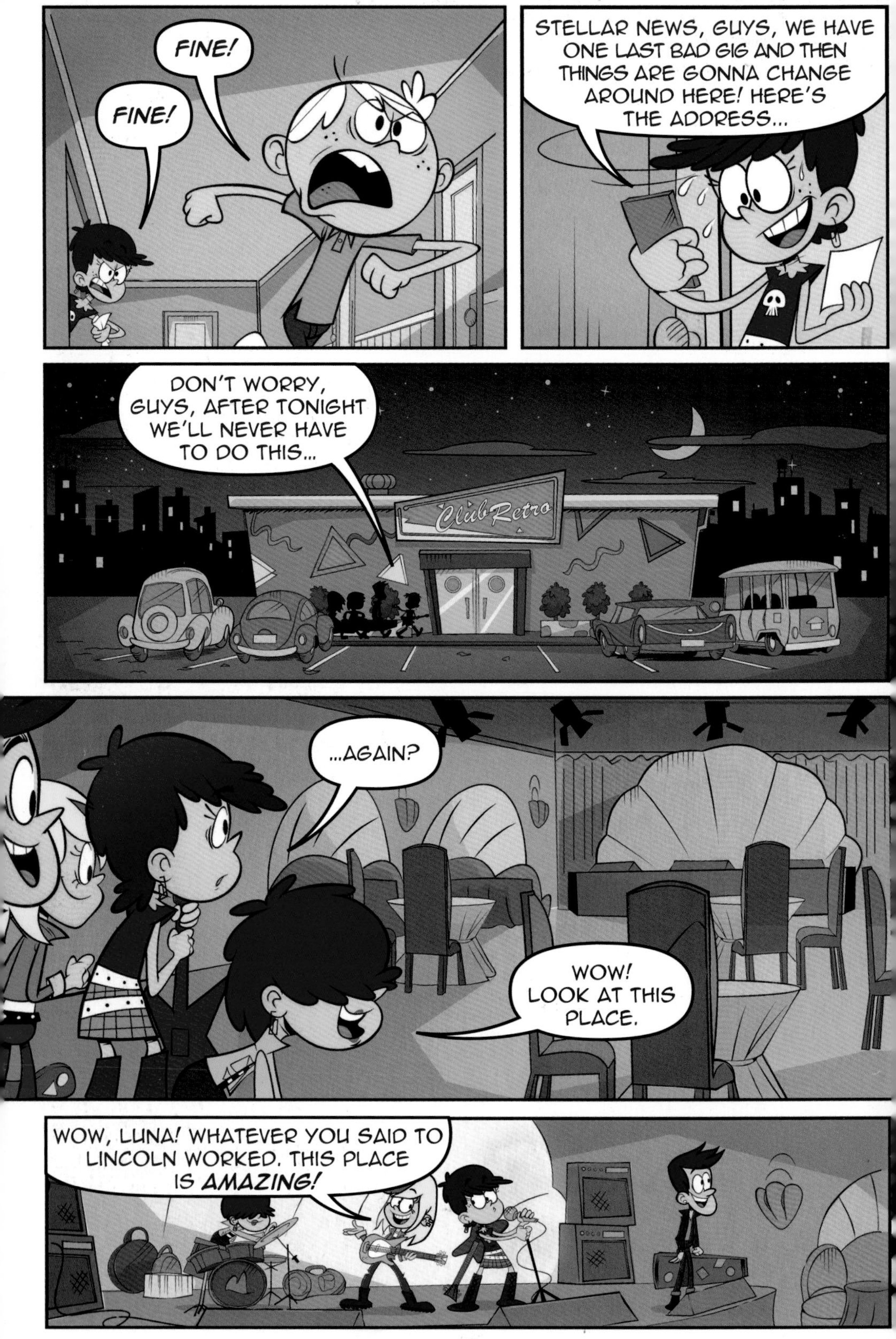
FINE!
FINE!
STELLAR NEWS, GUYS, WE HAVE ONE LAST BAD GIG AND THEN THINGS ARE GONNA CHANGE AROUND HERE! HERE'S THE ADDRESS...
DON'T WORRY, GUYS, AFTER TONIGHT WE'LL NEVER HAVE TO DO THIS...
Club Retro
...AGAIN?
WOW! LOOK AT THIS PLACE.
WOW, LUNA! WHATEVER YOU SAID TO LINCOLN WORKED. THIS PLACE IS AMAZING!

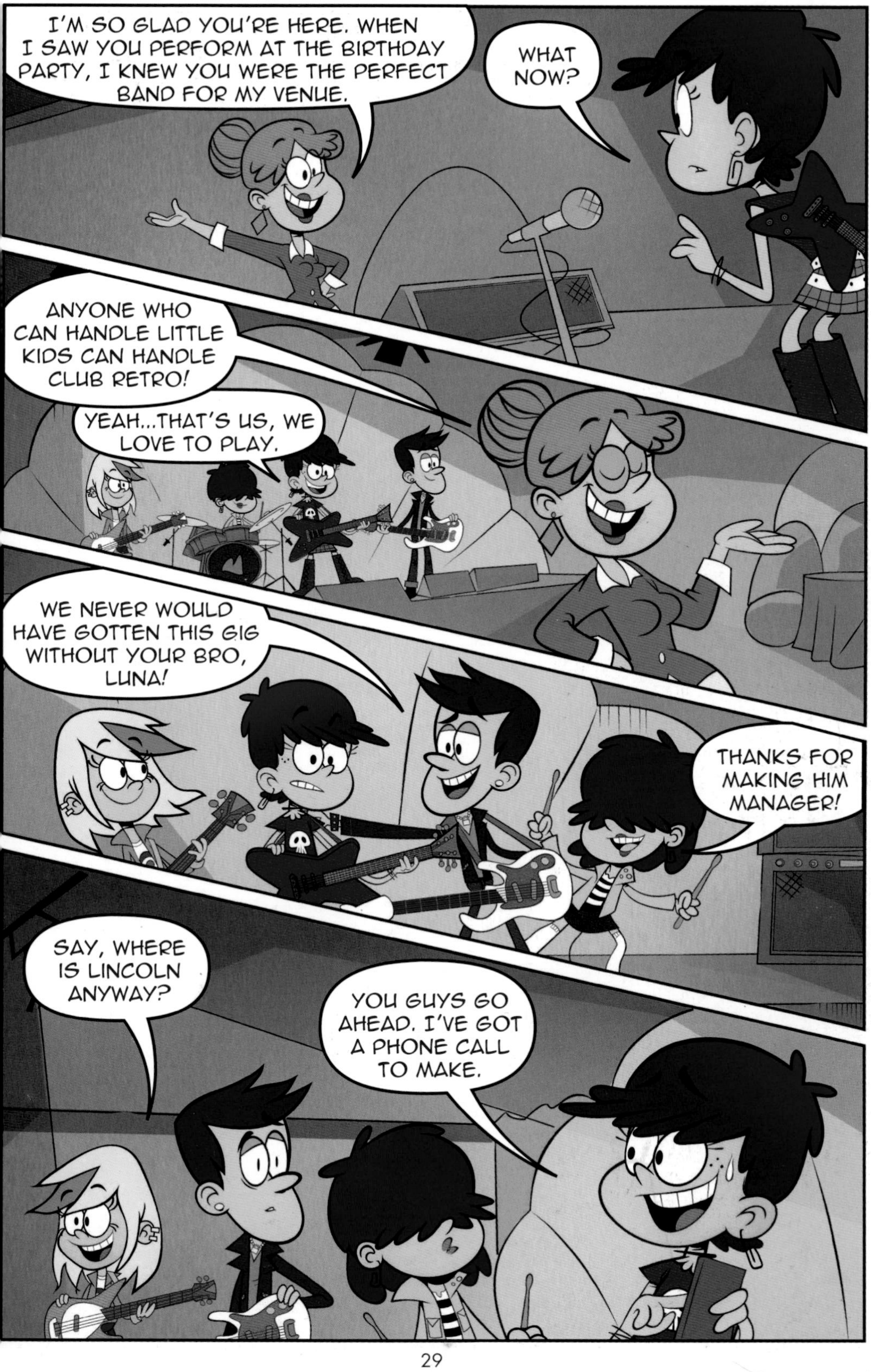
I'M SO GLAD YOU'RE HERE. WHEN I SAW YOU PERFORM AT THE BIRTHDAY PARTY, I KNEW YOU WERE THE PERFECT BAND FOR MY VENUE.
WHAT NOW?
ANYONE WHO CAN HANDLE LITTLE KIDS CAN HANDLE CLUB RETRO!
YEAH...THAT'S US, WE LOVE TO PLAY.
WE NEVER WOULD HAVE GOTTEN THIS GIG WITHOUT YOUR BRO, LUNA!
THANKS FOR MAKING HIM MANAGER!
SAY, WHERE IS LINCOLN ANYWAY?
YOU GUYS GO AHEAD. I'VE GOT A PHONE CALL TO MAKE.

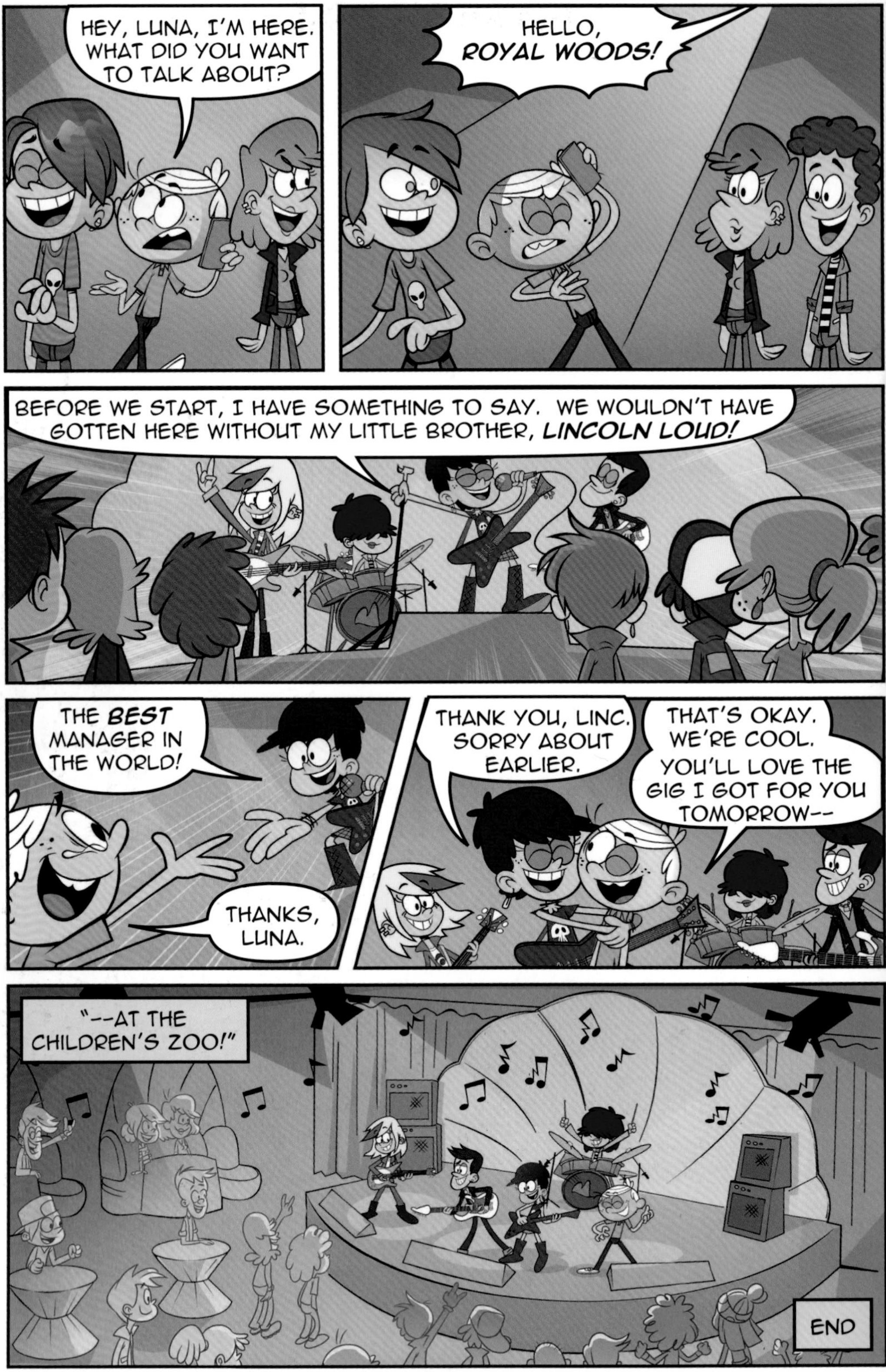
HEY, LUNA, I'M HERE. WHAT DID YOU WANT TO TALK ABOUT?
HELLO, ROYAL WOODS!
BEFORE WE START, I HAVE SOMETHING TO SAY. WE WOULDN'T HAVE GOTTEN HERE WITHOUT MY LITTLE BROTHER, LINCOLN LOUD!
THE BEST MANAGER IN THE WORLD!
THANKS, LUNA.
THANK YOU, LINC. SORRY ABOUT EARLIER.
THAT'S OKAY. WE'RE COOL. YOU'LL LOVE THE GIG I GOT FOR YOU TOMORROW--
"--AT THE CHILDREN'S ZOO!"
END

"FACE VALUE"

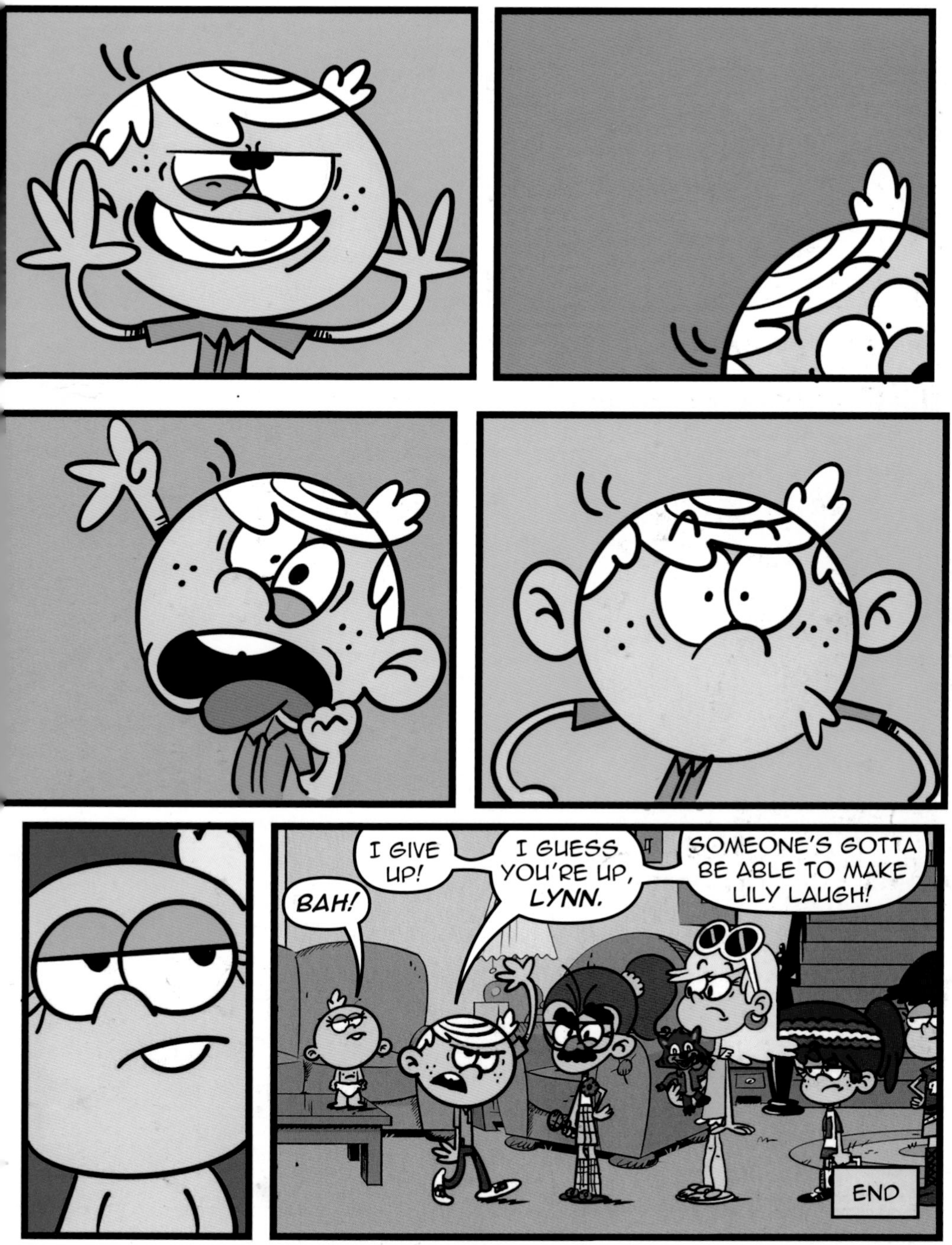
BAH!
I GIVE UP!
I GUESS YOU'RE UP, LYNN.
SOMEONE'S GOTTA BE ABLE TO MAKE LILY LAUGH!
END

"IMPROMPTOOT CONCERT"

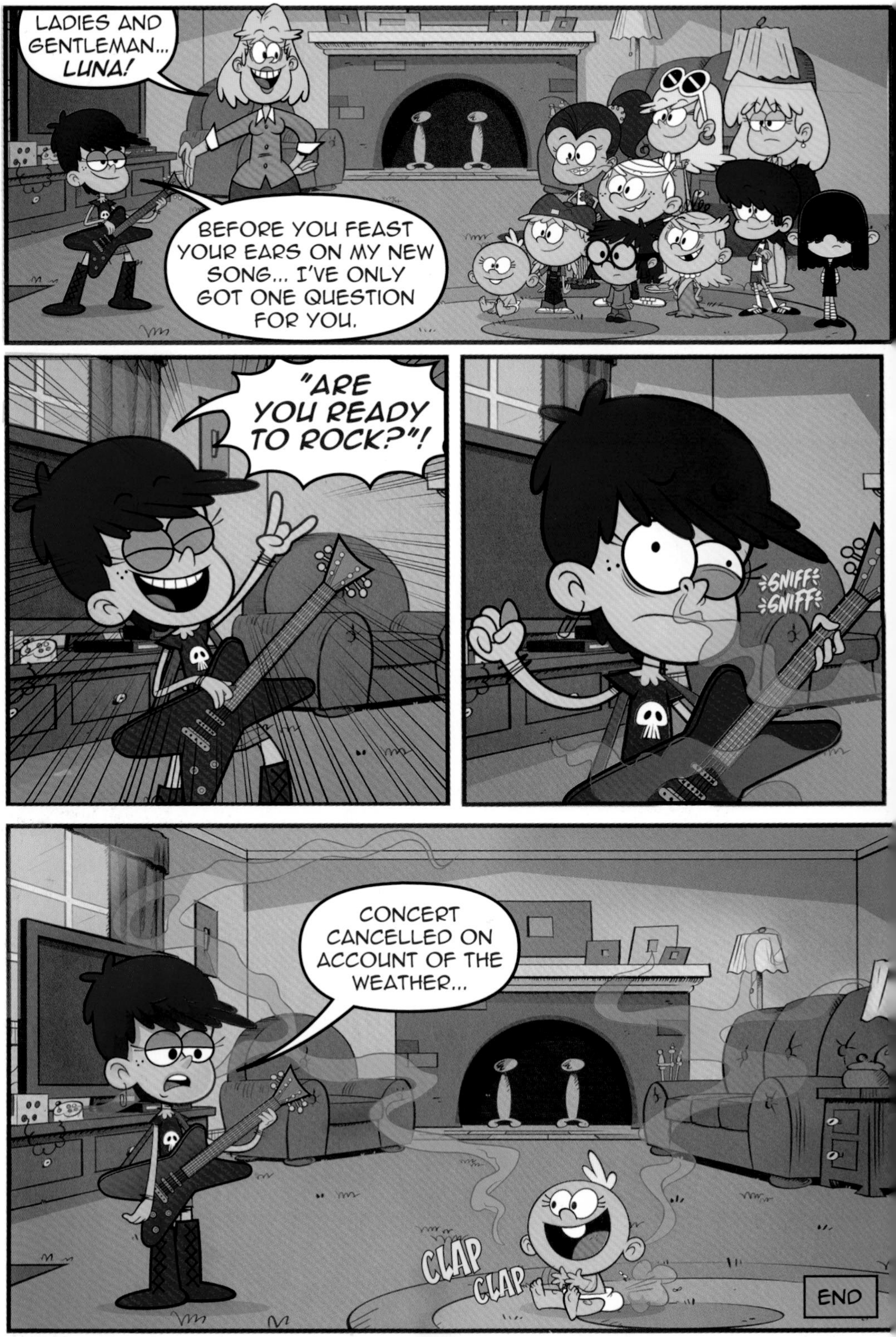

LADIES AND GENTLEMAN... LUNA!
BEFORE YOU FEAST YOUR EARS ON MY NEW SONG... I'VE ONLY GOT ONE QUESTION FOR YOU.
"ARE YOU READY TO ROCK?"!
SNIFF SNIFF
CONCERT CANCELLED ON ACCOUNT OF THE WEATHER...
CLAP CLAP
END

"CRUMBINAL JUSTICE"

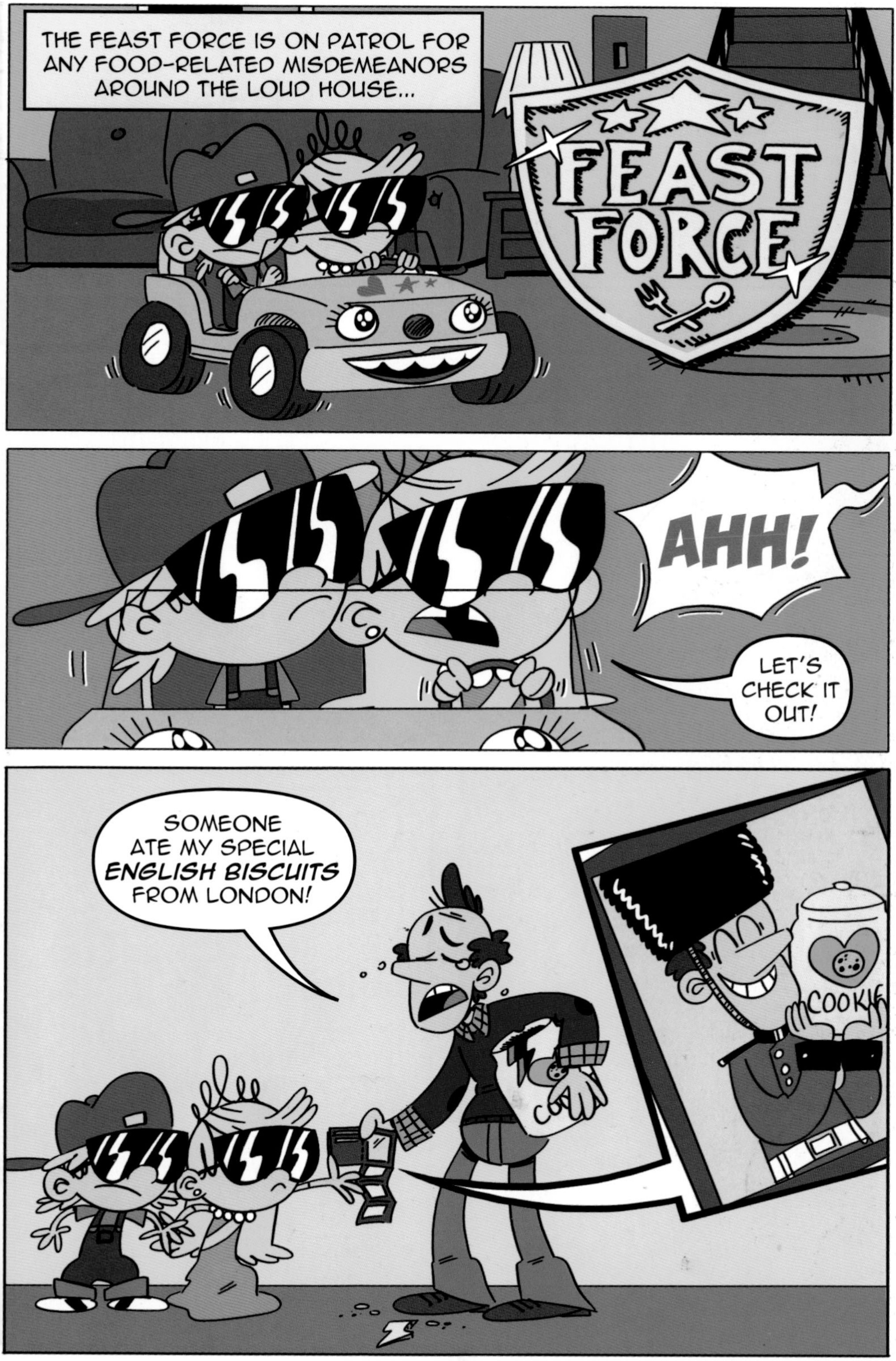
THE FEAST FORCE IS ON PATROL FOR ANY FOOD-RELATED MISDEMEANORS AROUND THE LOUD HOUSE...
FEAST FORCE
AHH!
LET'S CHECK IT OUT!
SOMEONE ATE MY SPECIAL *ENGLISH BISCUITS* FROM LONDON!
COOKIE

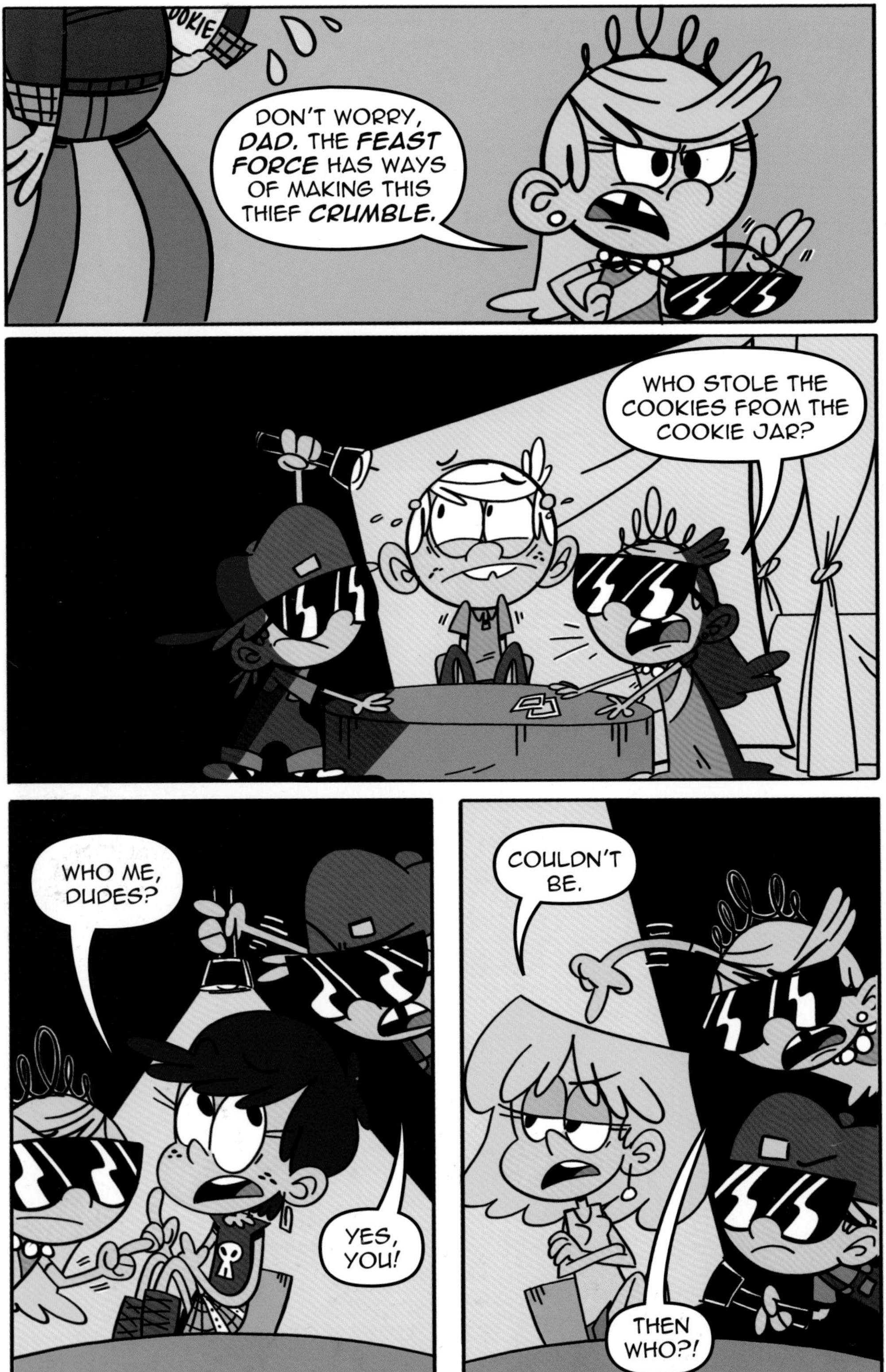
COOKIE
DON'T WORRY, DAD. THE FEAST FORCE HAS WAYS OF MAKING THIS THIEF CRUMBLE.
WHO STOLE THE COOKIES FROM THE COOKIE JAR?
WHO ME, DUDES?
YES, YOU!
COULDN'T BE.
THEN WHO?!

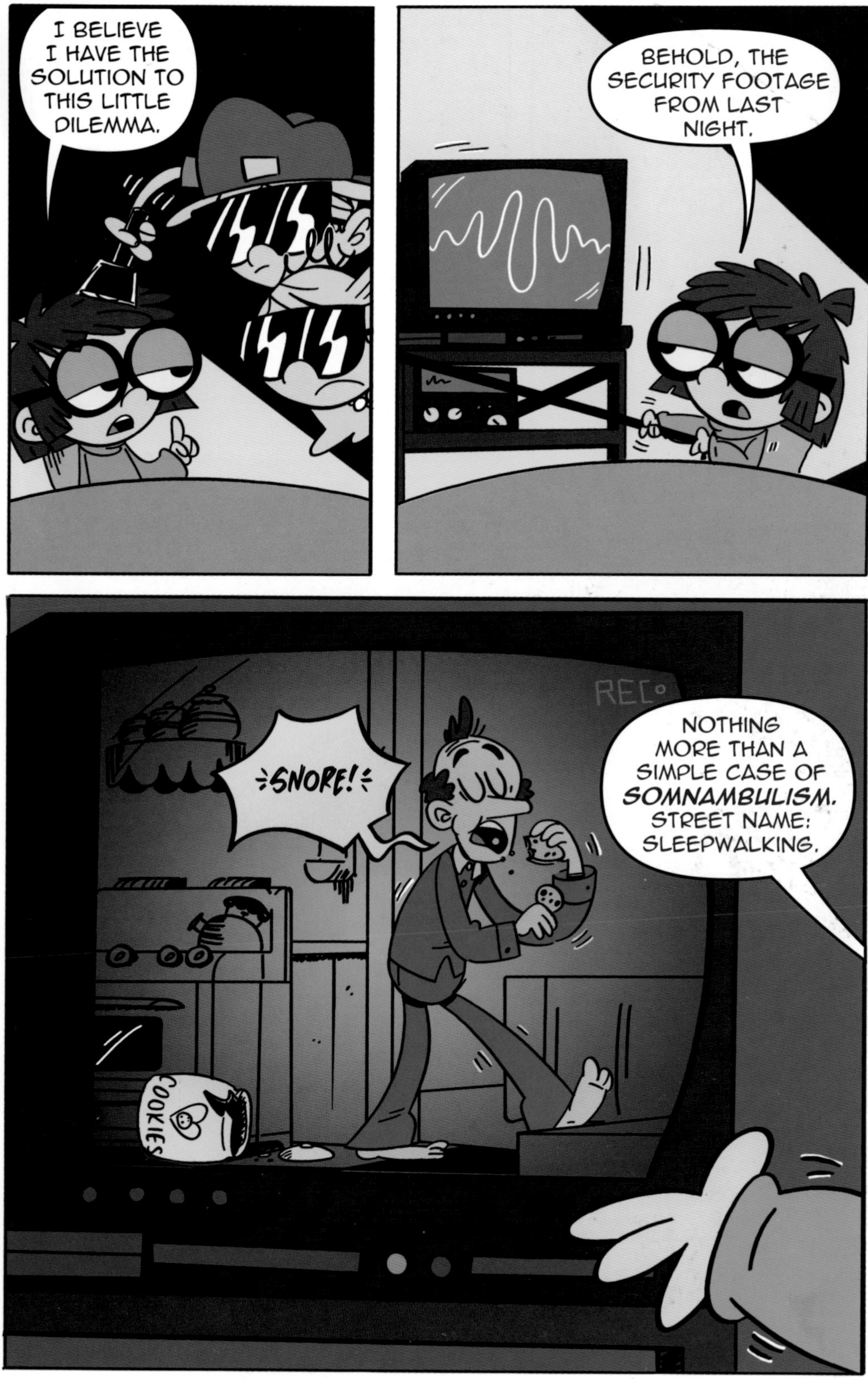
I BELIEVE I HAVE THE SOLUTION TO THIS LITTLE DILEMMA.
BEHOLD, THE SECURITY FOOTAGE FROM LAST NIGHT.
REC
SNORE!
NOTHING MORE THAN A SIMPLE CASE OF SOMNAMBULISM. STREET NAME: SLEEPWALKING.
COOKIES

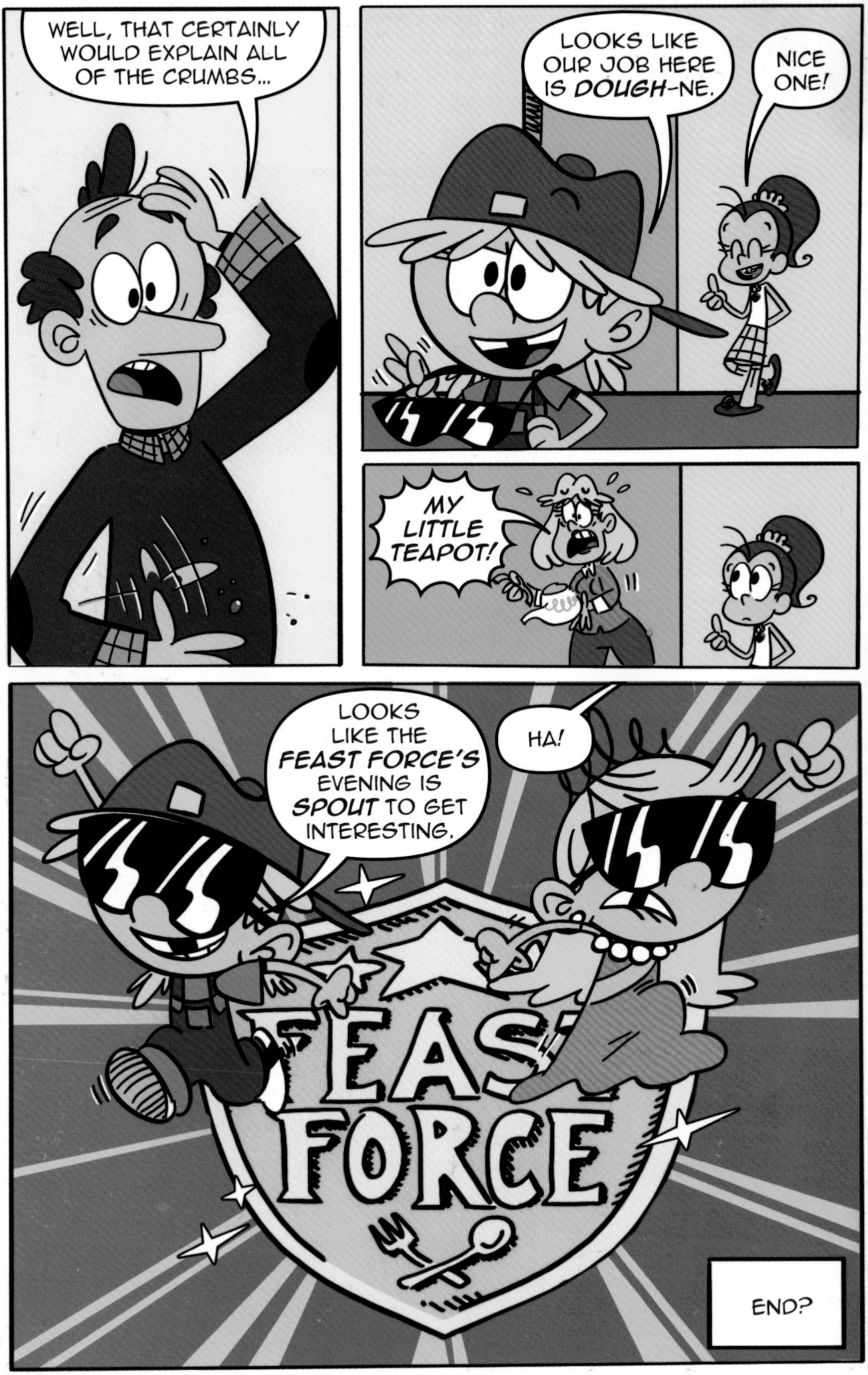

WELL, THAT CERTAINLY WOULD EXPLAIN ALL OF THE CRUMBS...
LOOKS LIKE OUR JOB HERE IS DOUGH-NE.
NICE ONE!
MY LITTLE TEAPOT!
LOOKS LIKE THE FEAST FORCE'S EVENING IS SPOUT TO GET INTERESTING.
HA!
FEAST FORCE
END?

"LOW ACHIEVEMENT"

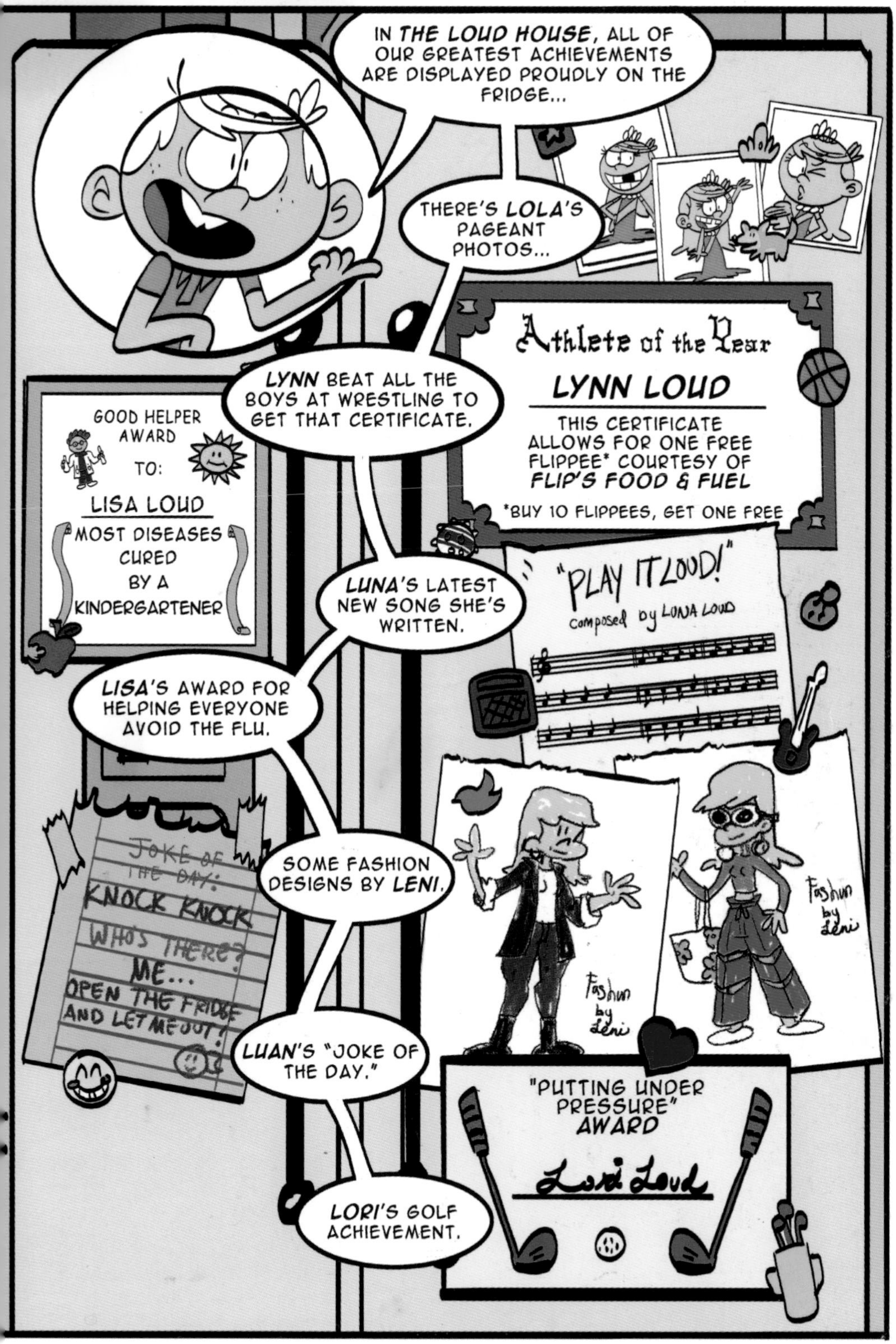

IN THE LOUD HOUSE, ALL OF OUR GREATEST ACHIEVEMENTS ARE DISPLAYED PROUDLY ON THE FRIDGE...
THERE'S LOLA'S PAGEANT PHOTOS...
Athlete of the Year
LYNN LOUD
THIS CERTIFICATE ALLOWS FOR ONE FREE FLIPPEE* COURTESY OF FLIP'S FOOD & FUEL
*BUY 10 FLIPPEES, GET ONE FREE
LYNN BEAT ALL THE BOYS AT WRESTLING TO GET THAT CERTIFICATE.
GOOD HELPER AWARD
TO:
LISA LOUD
MOST DISEASES CURED BY A KINDERGARTENER
"PLAY IT LOUD!"
composed by LUNA LOUD
LUNA'S LATEST NEW SONG SHE'S WRITTEN.
LISA'S AWARD FOR HELPING EVERYONE AVOID THE FLU.
JOKE OF THE DAY:
KNOCK KNOCK
WHO'S THERE?
ME...
OPEN THE FRIDGE AND LET ME OUT!
SOME FASHION DESIGNS BY LENI.
Fashun by Leni
Fashun by Leni
LUAN'S "JOKE OF THE DAY."
"PUTTING UNDER PRESSURE" AWARD
Lori Loud
LORI'S GOLF ACHIEVEMENT.

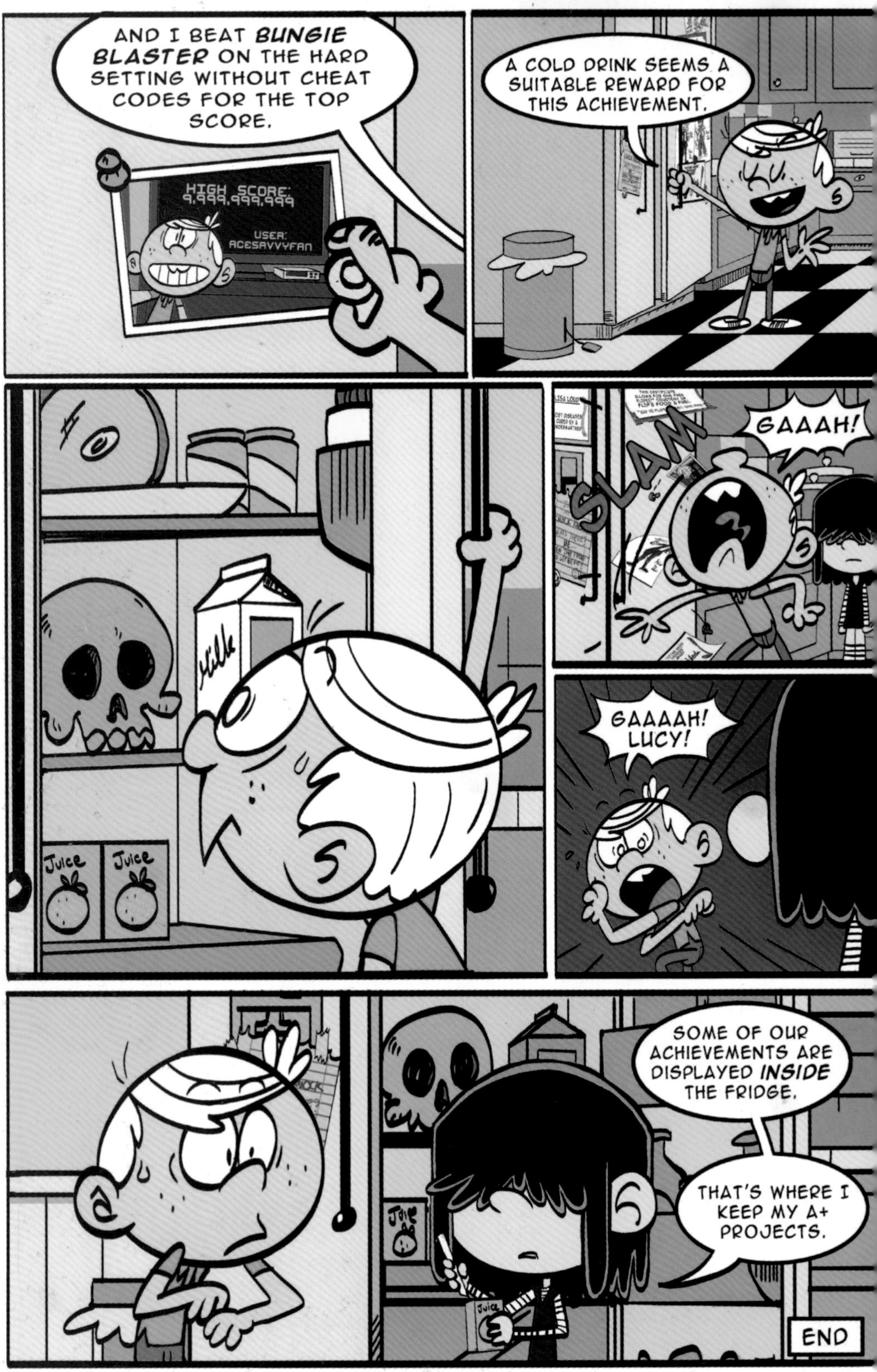
AND I BEAT *BUNGIE BLASTER* ON THE HARD SETTING WITHOUT CHEAT CODES FOR THE TOP SCORE.
HIGH SCORE:
9,999,999,999
USER:
ACESAVVYFAN
A COLD DRINK SEEMS A SUITABLE REWARD FOR THIS ACHIEVEMENT.
Milk
Juice
Juice
SLAM
GAAAH!
GAAAAH! LUCY!
SOME OF OUR ACHIEVEMENTS ARE DISPLAYED *INSIDE* THE FRIDGE.
THAT'S WHERE I KEEP MY A+ PROJECTS.
END

"THE LOUD HOUSE GAMES!"

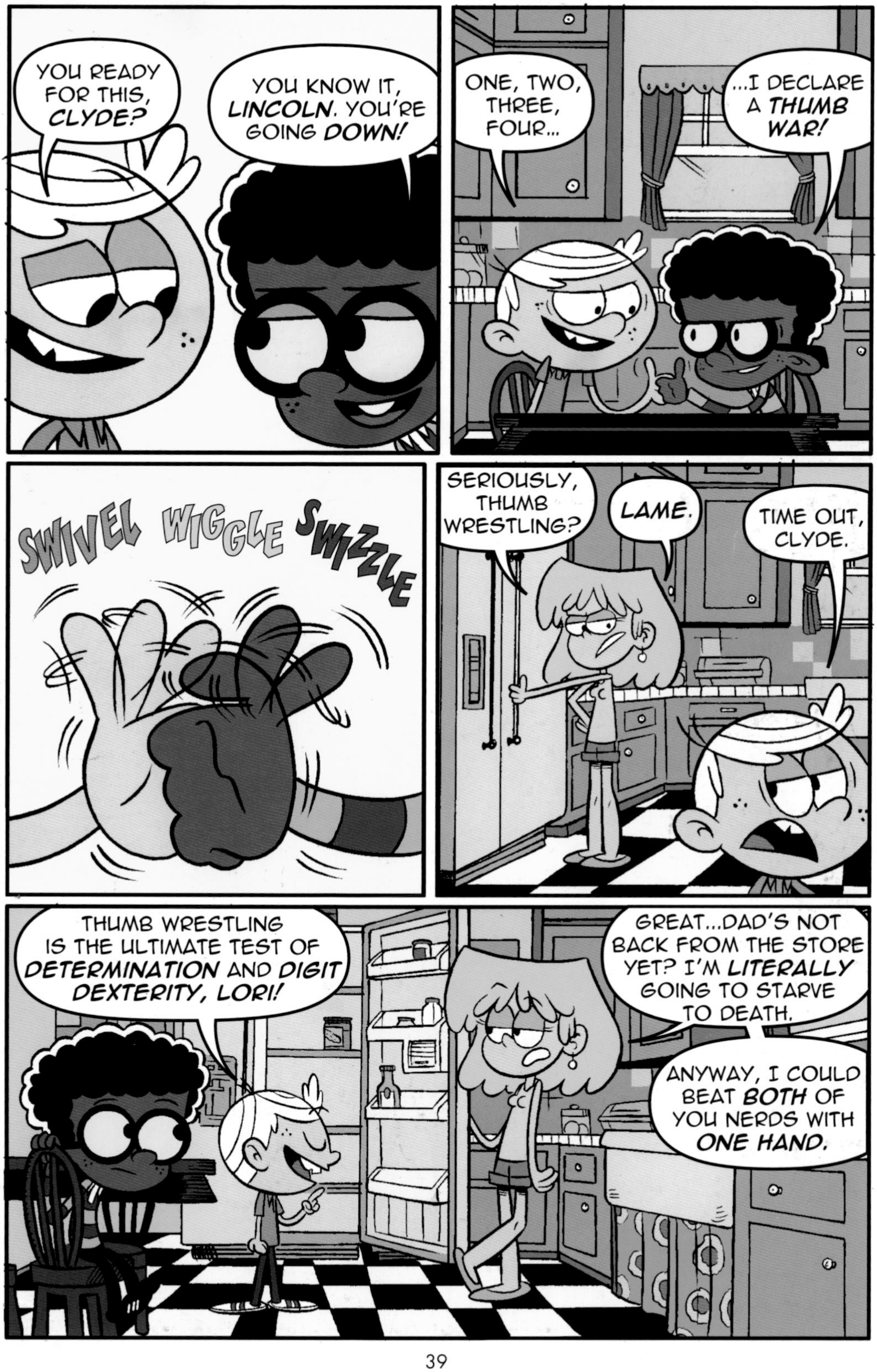
YOU READY FOR THIS, CLYDE?
YOU KNOW IT, LINCOLN. YOU'RE GOING DOWN!
ONE, TWO, THREE, FOUR...
...I DECLARE A THUMB WAR!
SWIVEL WIGGLE SWIZZLE
SERIOUSLY, THUMB WRESTLING?
LAME.
TIME OUT, CLYDE.
THUMB WRESTLING IS THE ULTIMATE TEST OF DETERMINATION AND DIGIT DEXTERITY, LORI!
GREAT...DAD'S NOT BACK FROM THE STORE YET? I'M LITERALLY GOING TO STARVE TO DEATH.
ANYWAY, I COULD BEAT BOTH OF YOU NERDS WITH ONE HAND.

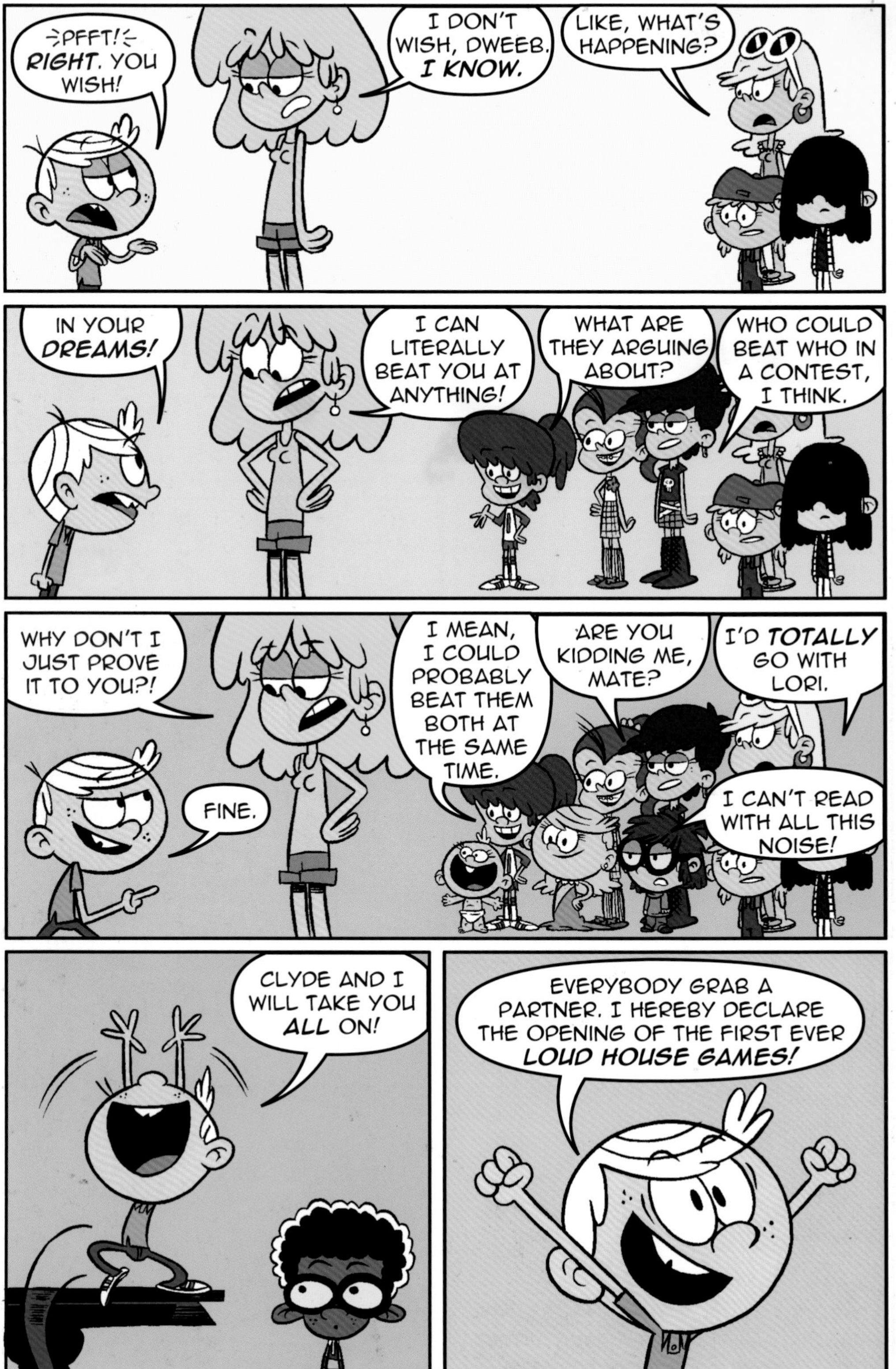
PFFT! RIGHT. YOU WISH!
I DON'T WISH, DWEEB. I KNOW.
LIKE, WHAT'S HAPPENING?
IN YOUR DREAMS!
I CAN LITERALLY BEAT YOU AT ANYTHING!
WHAT ARE THEY ARGUING ABOUT?
WHO COULD BEAT WHO IN A CONTEST, I THINK.
WHY DON'T I JUST PROVE IT TO YOU?!
FINE.
I MEAN, I COULD PROBABLY BEAT THEM BOTH AT THE SAME TIME.
ARE YOU KIDDING ME, MATE?
I'D TOTALLY GO WITH LORI.
I CAN'T READ WITH ALL THIS NOISE!
CLYDE AND I WILL TAKE YOU ALL ON!
EVERYBODY GRAB A PARTNER. I HEREBY DECLARE THE OPENING OF THE FIRST EVER LOUD HOUSE GAMES!

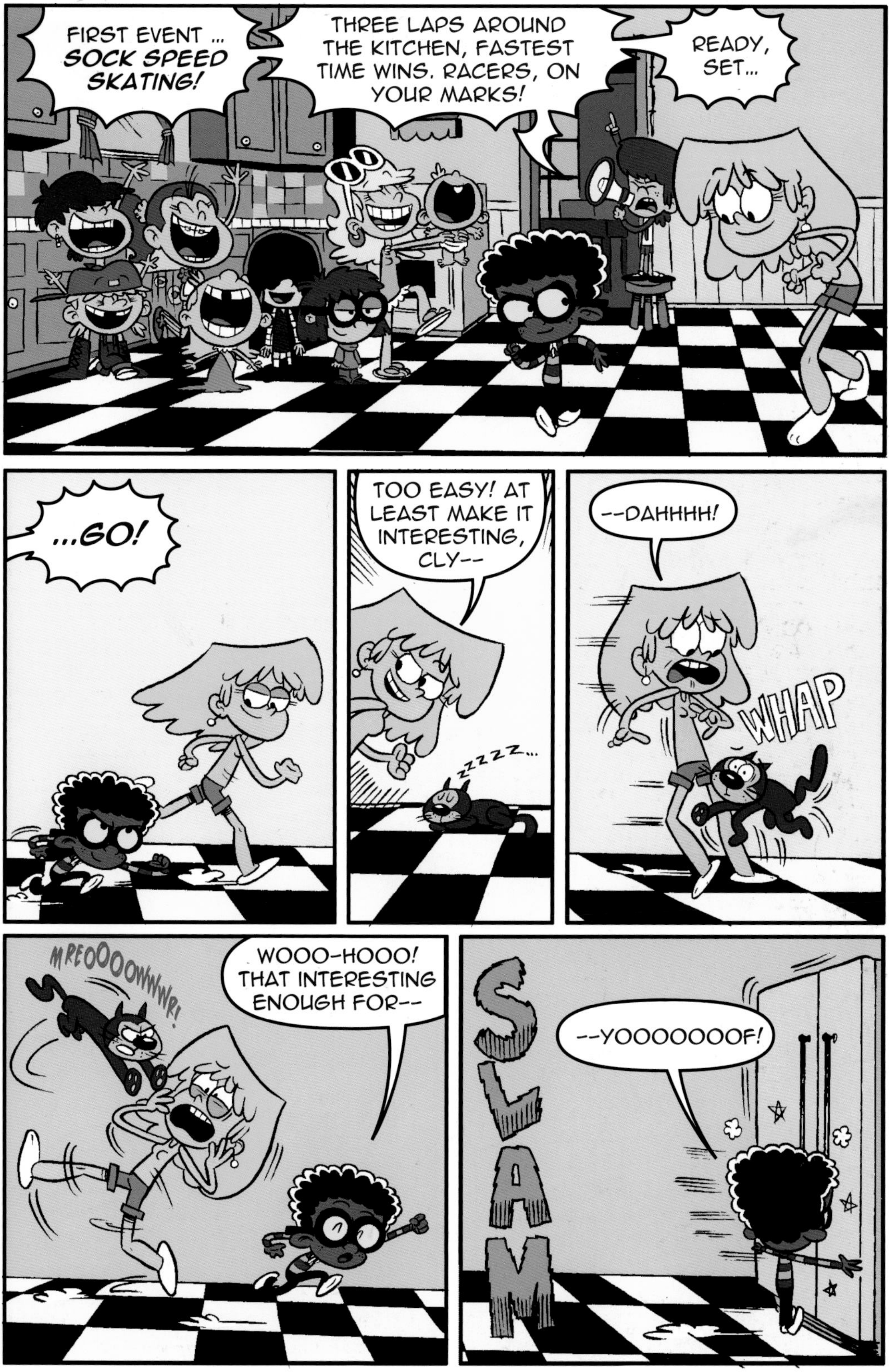
FIRST EVENT ... SOCK SPEED SKATING!
THREE LAPS AROUND THE KITCHEN, FASTEST TIME WINS. RACERS, ON YOUR MARKS!
READY, SET...
...GO!
TOO EASY! AT LEAST MAKE IT INTERESTING, CLY--
ZZZZZ...
--DAHHHH!
WHAP
MREOOOOWWWR!
WOOO-HOOO! THAT INTERESTING ENOUGH FOR--
SLAM
--YOOOOOOOF!

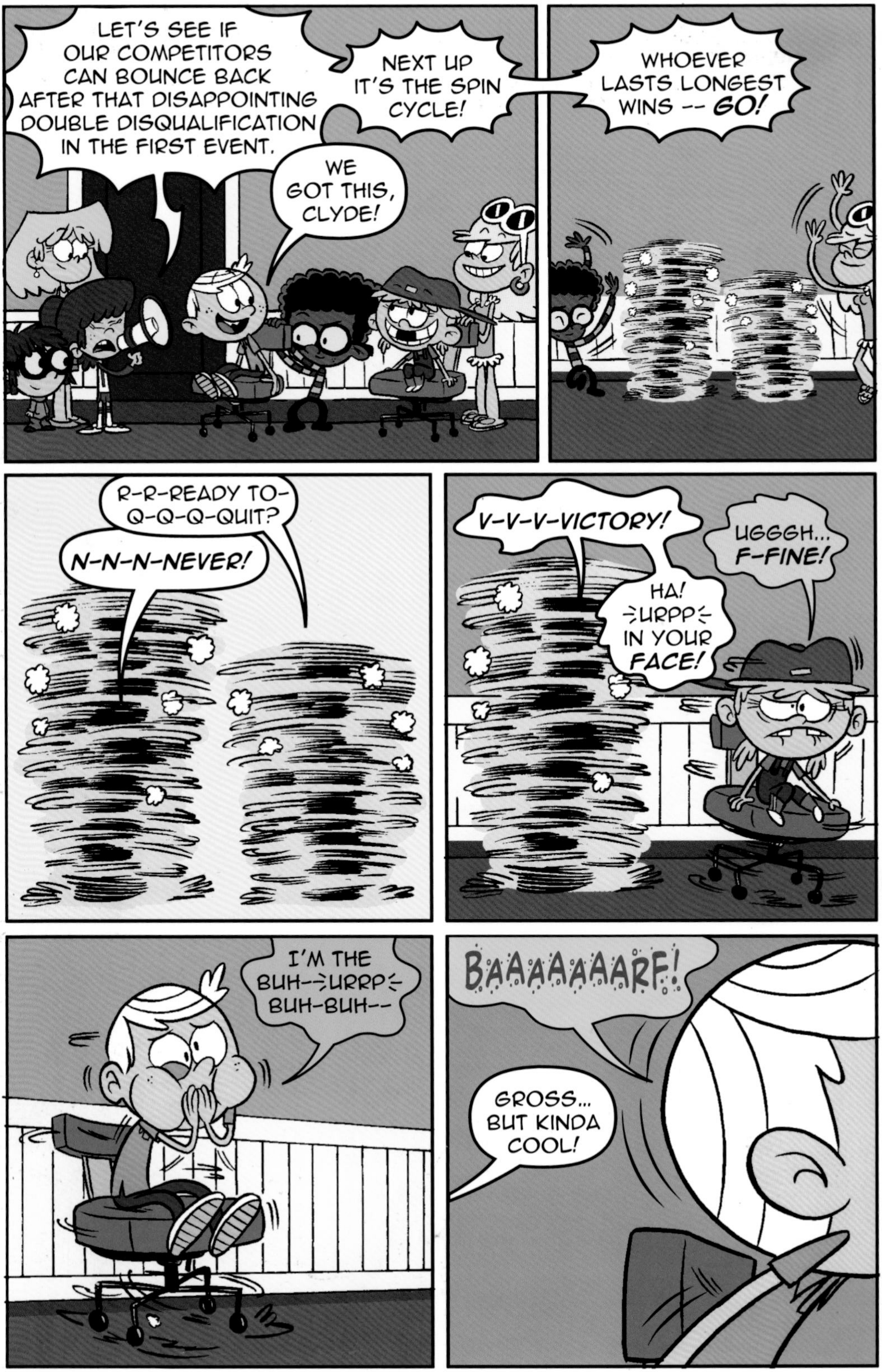
LET'S SEE IF OUR COMPETITORS CAN BOUNCE BACK AFTER THAT DISAPPOINTING DOUBLE DISQUALIFICATION IN THE FIRST EVENT.
NEXT UP IT'S THE SPIN CYCLE!
WE GOT THIS, CLYDE!
WHOEVER LASTS LONGEST WINS -- GO!
R-R-READY TO-Q-Q-Q-QUIT?
N-N-N-NEVER!
V-V-V-VICTORY!
HA! URPP IN YOUR FACE!
UGGGH... F-FINE!
I'M THE BUH-URRP BUH-BUH--
BAAAAAAARF!
GROSS... BUT KINDA COOL!

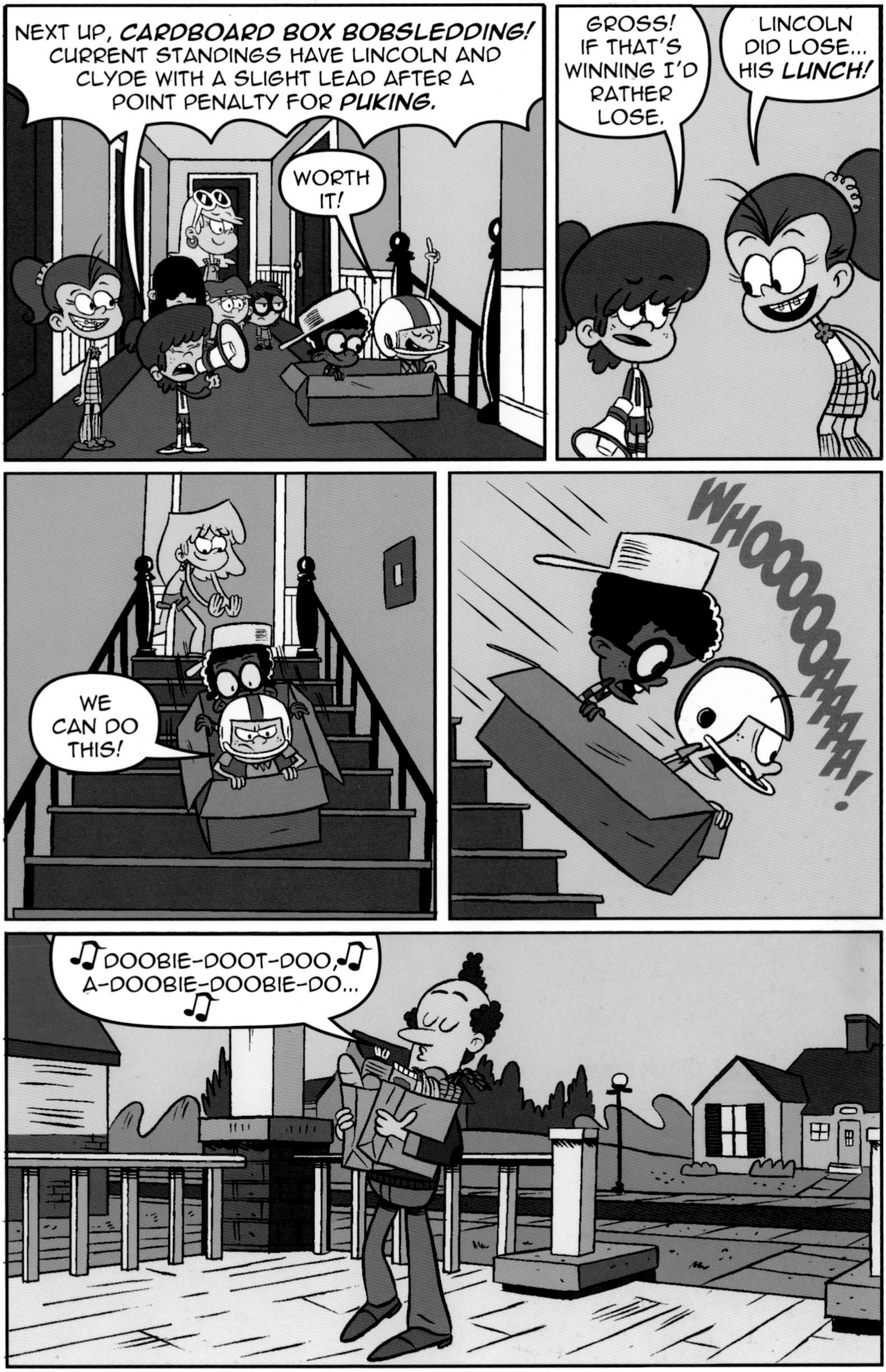
NEXT UP, CARDBOARD BOX BOBSLEDDING! CURRENT STANDINGS HAVE LINCOLN AND CLYDE WITH A SLIGHT LEAD AFTER A POINT PENALTY FOR PUKING.
WORTH IT!
GROSS! IF THAT'S WINNING I'D RATHER LOSE.
LINCOLN DID LOSE... HIS LUNCH!
WE CAN DO THIS!
WHOOOOAAAA!
DOOBIE-DOOT-DOO, A-DOOBIE-DOOBIE-DO...

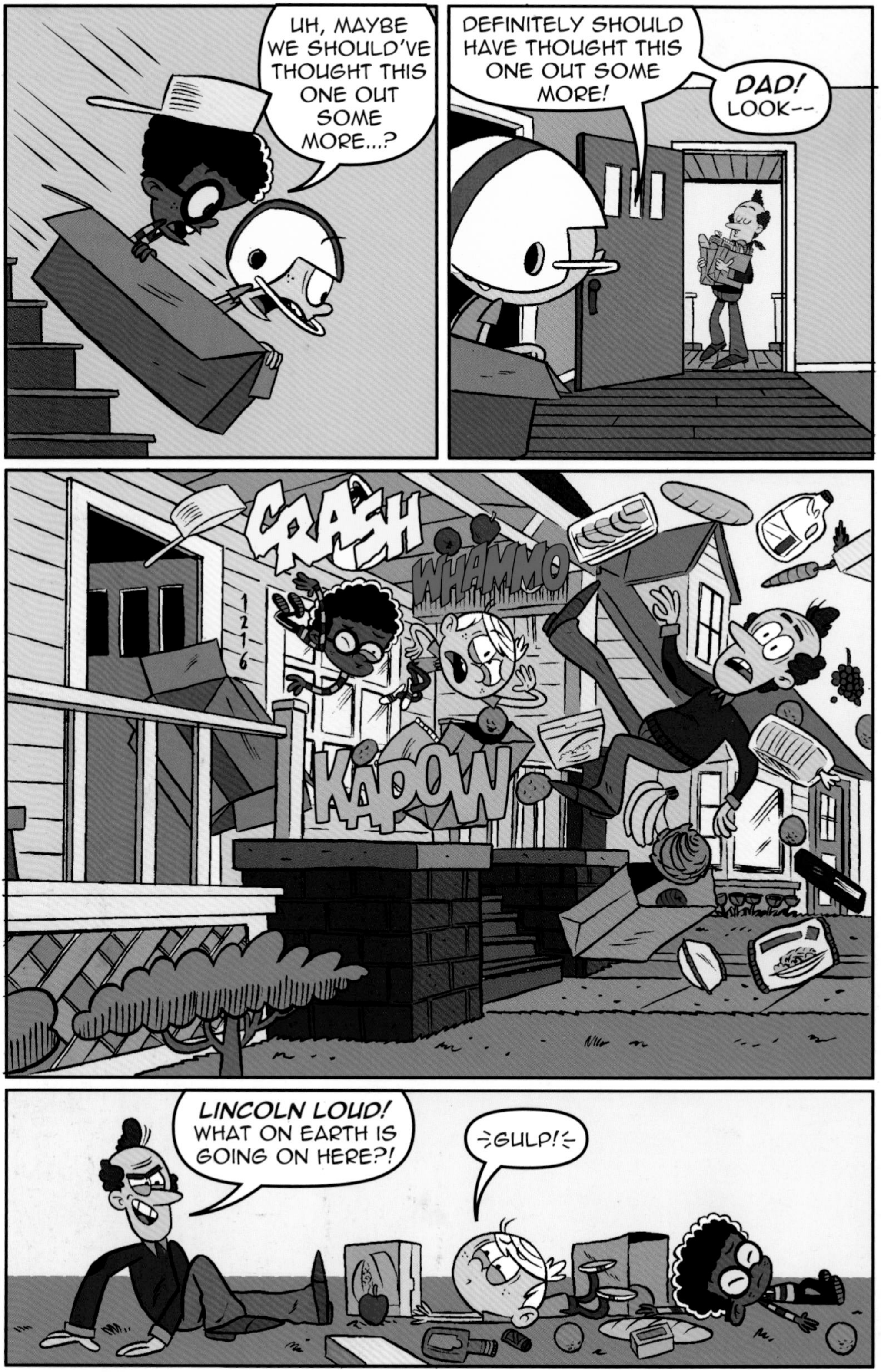
UH, MAYBE WE SHOULD'VE THOUGHT THIS ONE OUT SOME MORE...?
DEFINITELY SHOULD HAVE THOUGHT THIS ONE OUT SOME MORE!
DAD! LOOK--
CRASH
WHAMMO
KAPOW
1216
LINCOLN LOUD! WHAT ON EARTH IS GOING ON HERE?!
GULP!

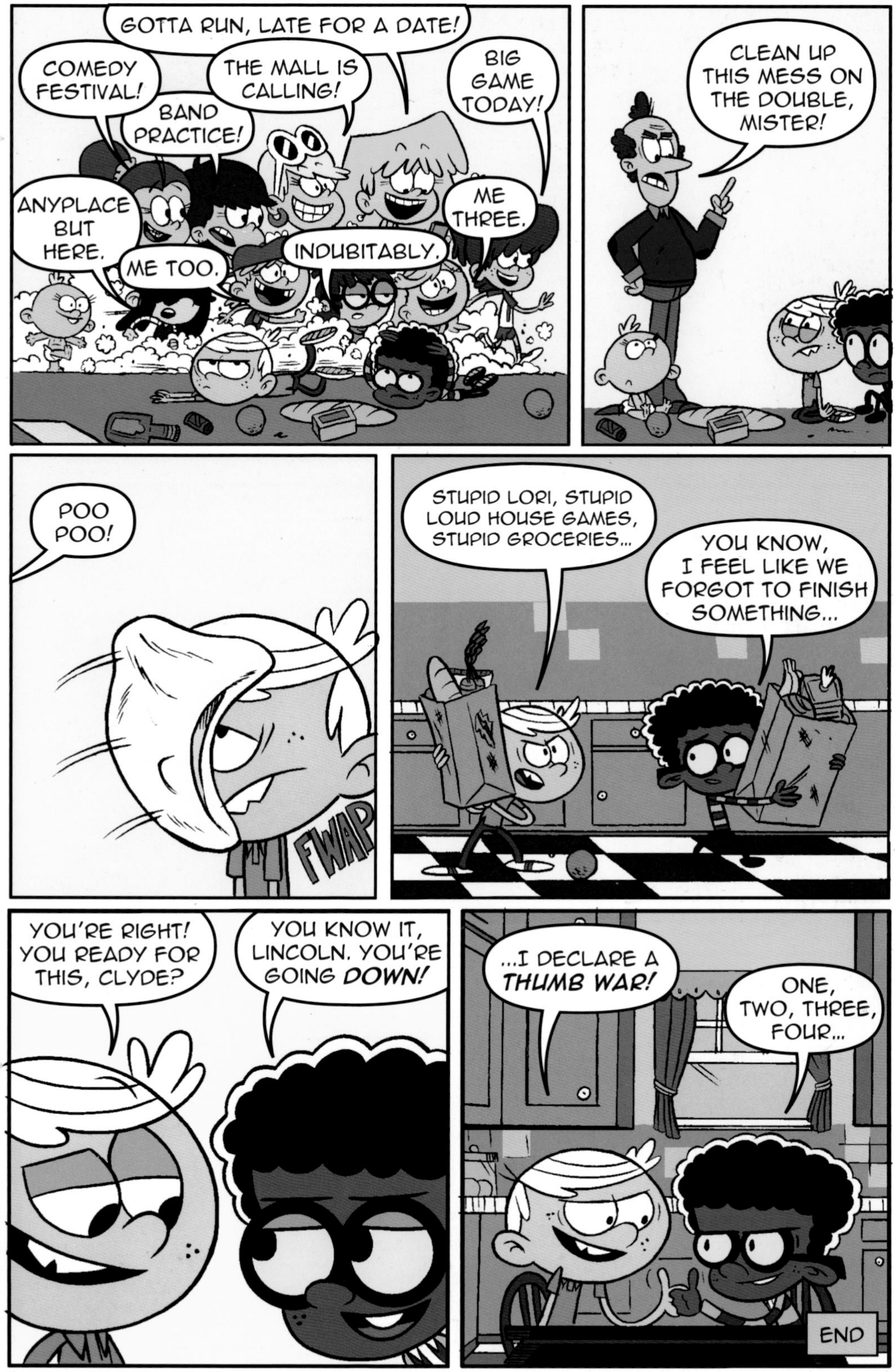
GOTTA RUN, LATE FOR A DATE!
COMEDY FESTIVAL!
BAND PRACTICE!
THE MALL IS CALLING!
BIG GAME TODAY!
ANYPLACE BUT HERE.
ME TOO.
INDUBITABLY.
ME THREE.
CLEAN UP THIS MESS ON THE DOUBLE, MISTER!
POO POO!
FWAP
STUPID LORI, STUPID LOUD HOUSE GAMES, STUPID GROCERIES...
YOU KNOW, I FEEL LIKE WE FORGOT TO FINISH SOMETHING...
YOU'RE RIGHT! YOU READY FOR THIS, CLYDE?
YOU KNOW IT, LINCOLN. YOU'RE GOING DOWN!
...I DECLARE A THUMB WAR!
ONE, TWO, THREE, FOUR...
END

"FIND OF THE CENTURY"

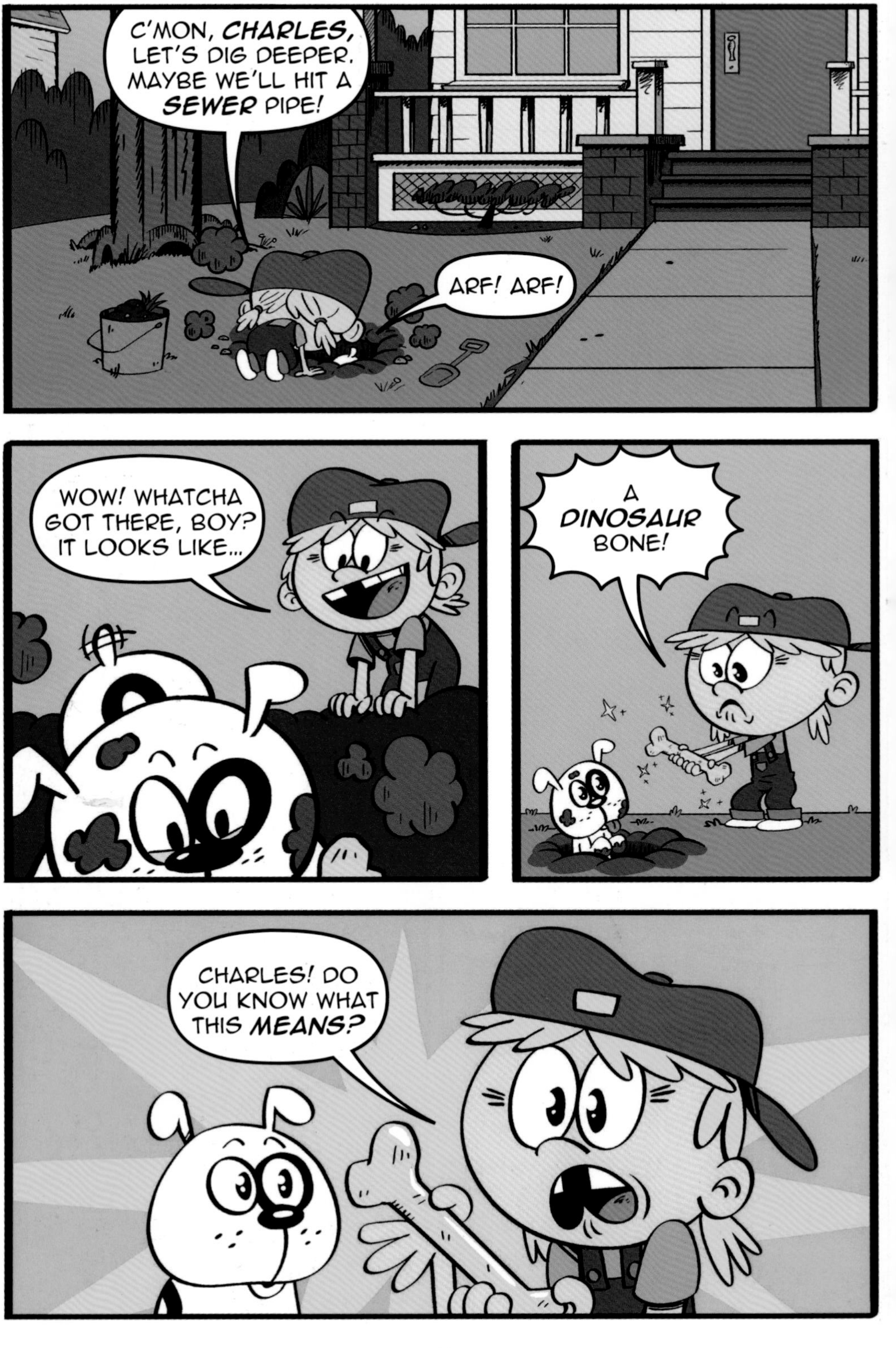
C'MON, CHARLES, LET'S DIG DEEPER. MAYBE WE'LL HIT A SEWER PIPE!
ARF! ARF!
WOW! WHATCHA GOT THERE, BOY? IT LOOKS LIKE...
A DINOSAUR BONE!
CHARLES! DO YOU KNOW WHAT THIS MEANS?

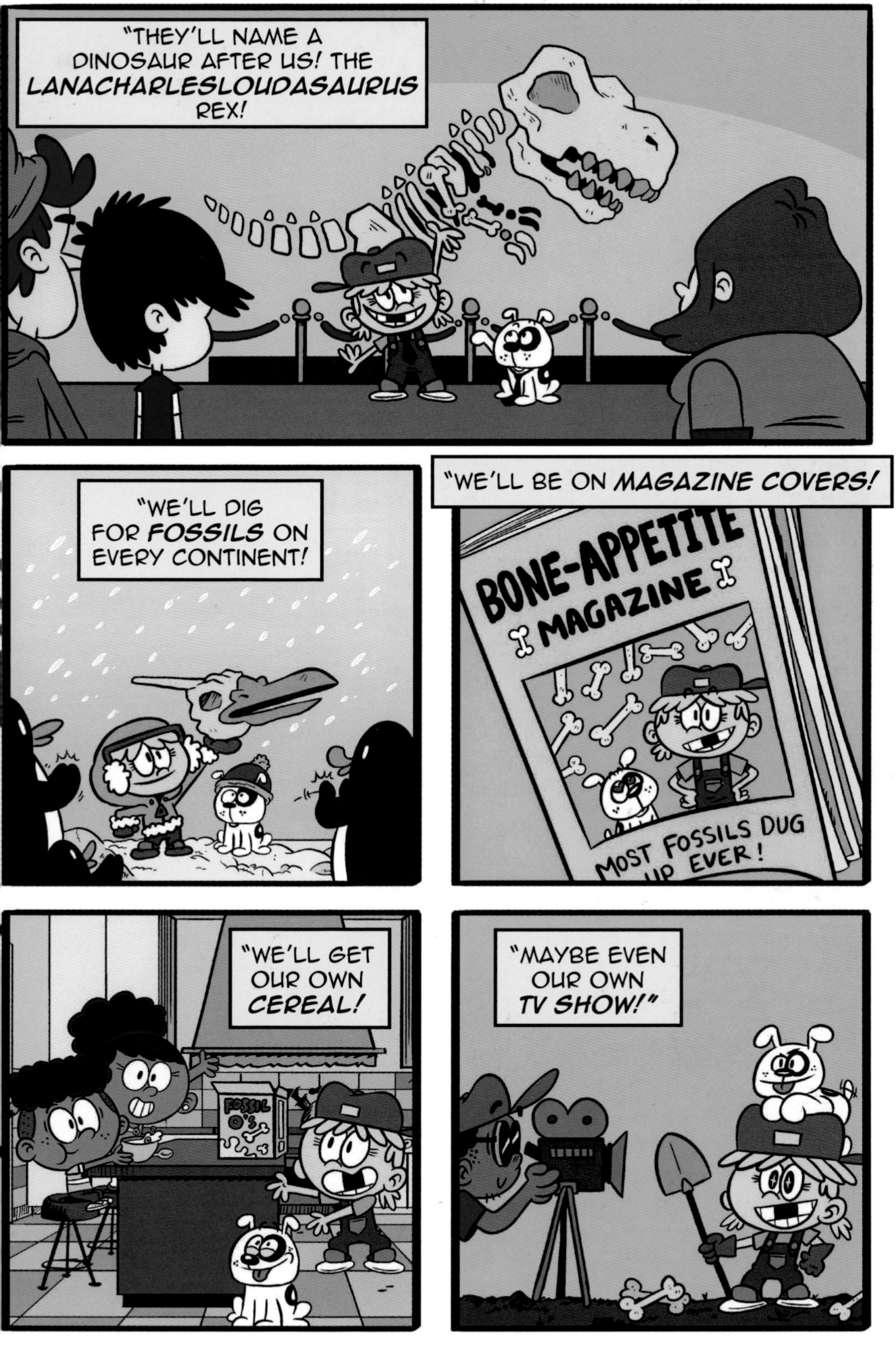
"THEY'LL NAME A DINOSAUR AFTER US! THE *LANACHARLESLOUDASAURUS* REX!
"WE'LL DIG FOR *FOSSILS* ON EVERY CONTINENT!
"WE'LL BE ON *MAGAZINE COVERS!*
BONE-APPETITE MAGAZINE
MOST FOSSILS DUG UP EVER!
"WE'LL GET OUR OWN *CEREAL!*
FOSSIL O'S
"MAYBE EVEN OUR OWN *TV SHOW!"*

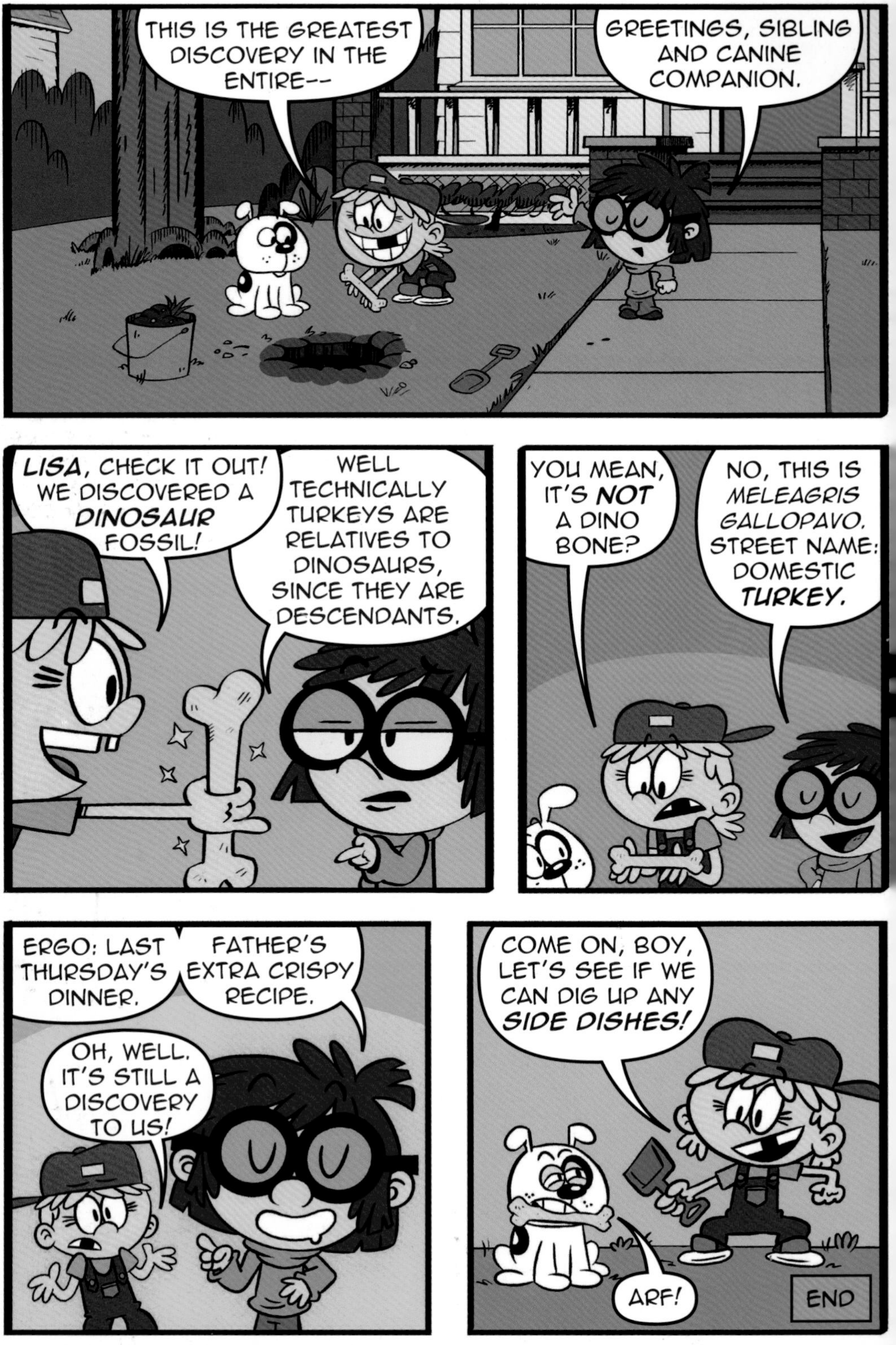
THIS IS THE GREATEST DISCOVERY IN THE ENTIRE--
GREETINGS, SIBLING AND CANINE COMPANION.
LISA, CHECK IT OUT! WE DISCOVERED A DINOSAUR FOSSIL!
WELL TECHNICALLY TURKEYS ARE RELATIVES TO DINOSAURS, SINCE THEY ARE DESCENDANTS.
YOU MEAN, IT'S NOT A DINO BONE?
NO, THIS IS MELEAGRIS GALLOPAVO. STREET NAME: DOMESTIC TURKEY.
ERGO: LAST THURSDAY'S DINNER.
FATHER'S EXTRA CRISPY RECIPE.
OH, WELL. IT'S STILL A DISCOVERY TO US!
COME ON, BOY, LET'S SEE IF WE CAN DIG UP ANY SIDE DISHES!
ARF!
END

"A MONSTER PLAN"

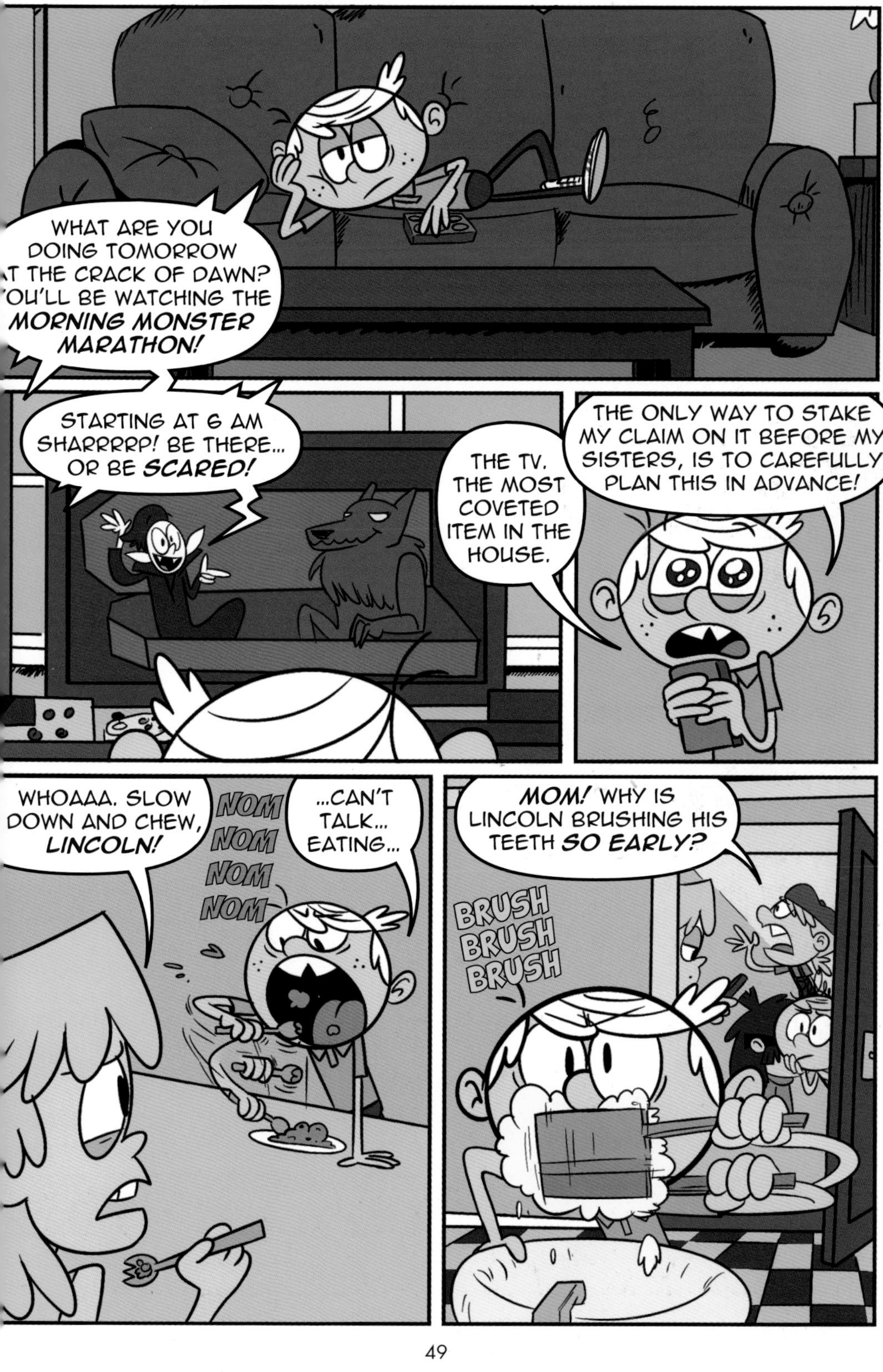

WHAT ARE YOU DOING TOMORROW AT THE CRACK OF DAWN? YOU'LL BE WATCHING THE MORNING MONSTER MARATHON!
STARTING AT 6 AM SHARRRRP! BE THERE... OR BE SCARED!
THE TV. THE MOST COVETED ITEM IN THE HOUSE.
THE ONLY WAY TO STAKE MY CLAIM ON IT BEFORE MY SISTERS, IS TO CAREFULLY PLAN THIS IN ADVANCE!
WHOAAA. SLOW DOWN AND CHEW, LINCOLN!
NOM NOM NOM NOM
...CAN'T TALK... EATING...
MOM! WHY IS LINCOLN BRUSHING HIS TEETH SO EARLY?
BRUSH BRUSH BRUSH

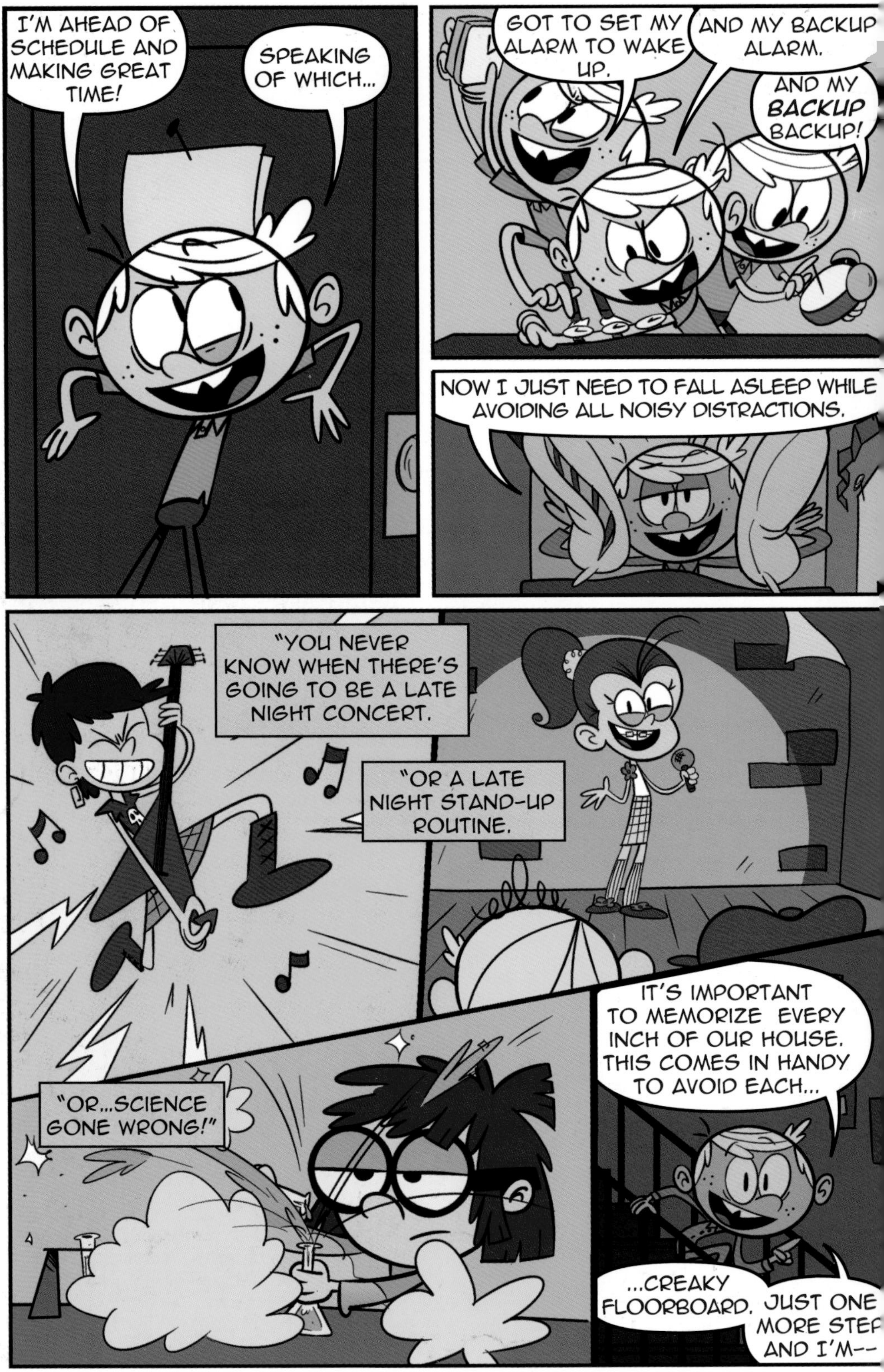
I'M AHEAD OF SCHEDULE AND MAKING GREAT TIME!
SPEAKING OF WHICH...
GOT TO SET MY ALARM TO WAKE UP.
AND MY BACKUP ALARM.
AND MY **BACKUP** BACKUP!
NOW I JUST NEED TO FALL ASLEEP WHILE AVOIDING ALL NOISY DISTRACTIONS.
"YOU NEVER KNOW WHEN THERE'S GOING TO BE A LATE NIGHT CONCERT.
"OR A LATE NIGHT STAND-UP ROUTINE.
"OR...SCIENCE GONE WRONG!"
IT'S IMPORTANT TO MEMORIZE EVERY INCH OF OUR HOUSE. THIS COMES IN HANDY TO AVOID EACH...
...CREAKY FLOORBOARD.
JUST ONE MORE STEP AND I'M--

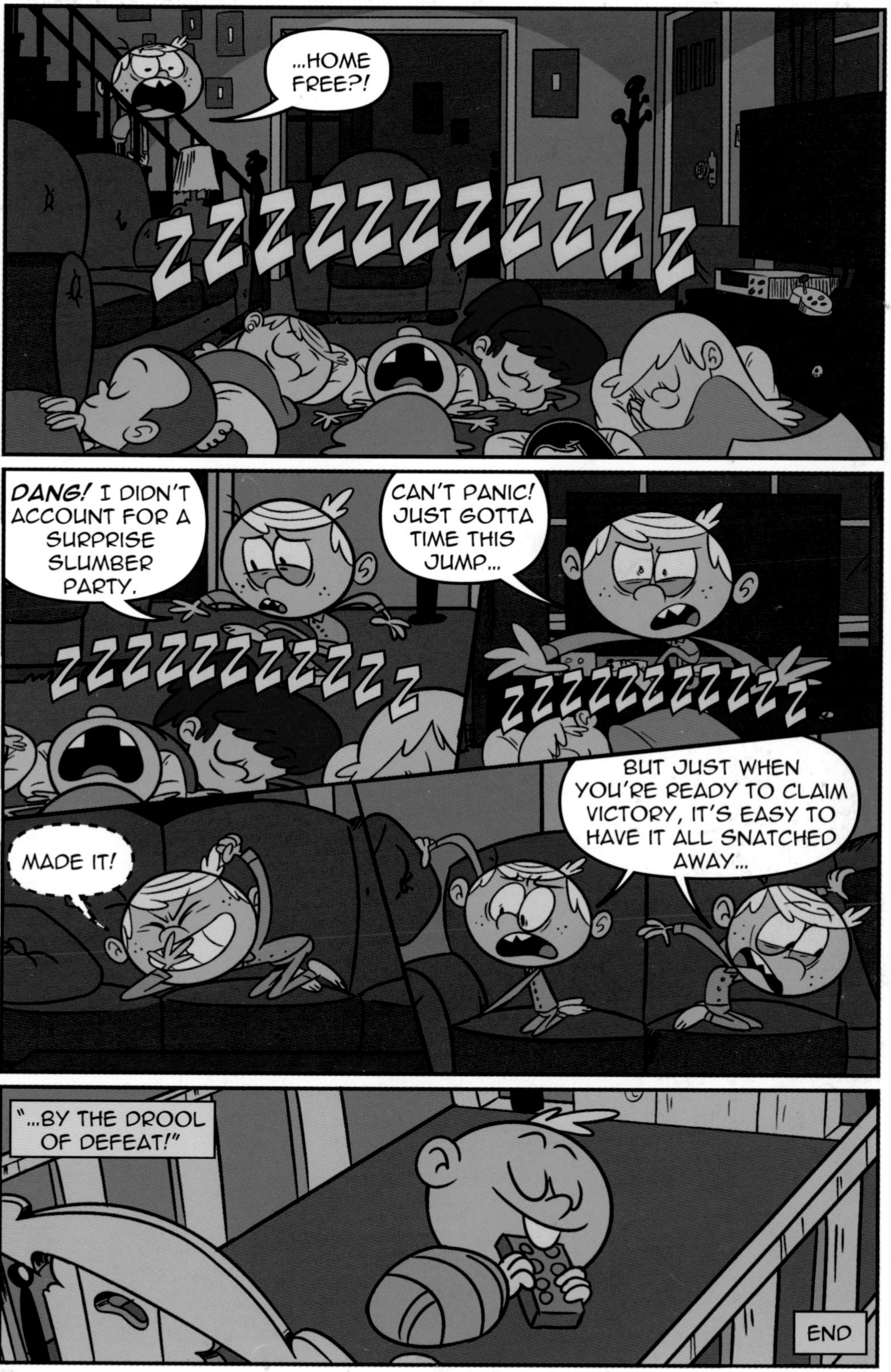

...HOME FREE?!
ZZZZZZZZZZZZZ
DANG! I DIDN'T ACCOUNT FOR A SURPRISE SLUMBER PARTY.
ZZZZZZZZZZZ
CAN'T PANIC! JUST GOTTA TIME THIS JUMP...
ZZZZZZZZZZZZZZ
MADE IT!
BUT JUST WHEN YOU'RE READY TO CLAIM VICTORY, IT'S EASY TO HAVE IT ALL SNATCHED AWAY...
"...BY THE DROOL OF DEFEAT!"
END

"Out of Tune"

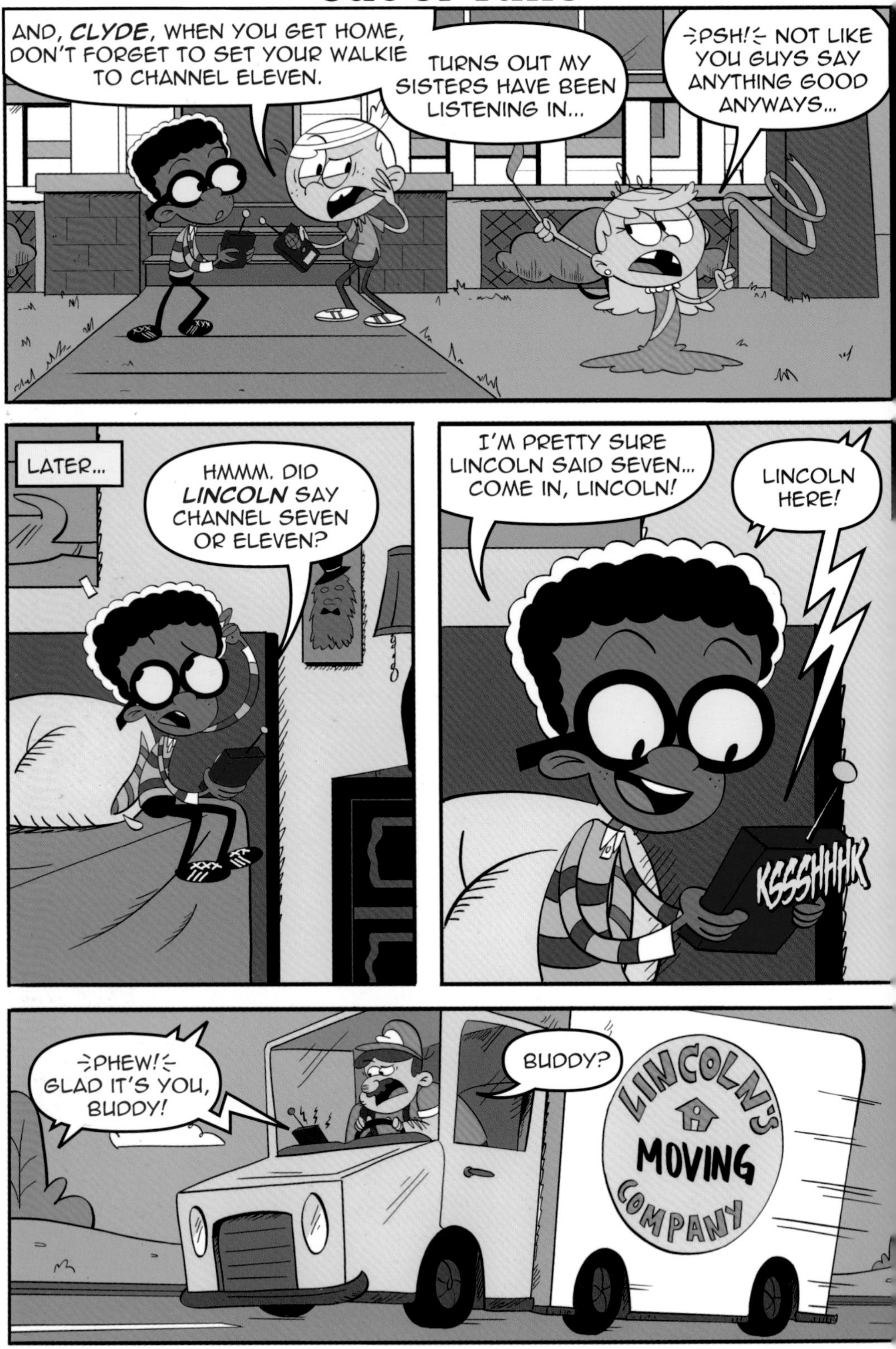
AND, CLYDE, WHEN YOU GET HOME, DON'T FORGET TO SET YOUR WALKIE TO CHANNEL ELEVEN.
TURNS OUT MY SISTERS HAVE BEEN LISTENING IN...
PSH! NOT LIKE YOU GUYS SAY ANYTHING GOOD ANYWAYS...
LATER...
HMMM. DID LINCOLN SAY CHANNEL SEVEN OR ELEVEN?
I'M PRETTY SURE LINCOLN SAID SEVEN... COME IN, LINCOLN!
LINCOLN HERE!
KSSSHHHK
PHEW! GLAD IT'S YOU, BUDDY!
BUDDY?
LINCOLN'S MOVING COMPANY

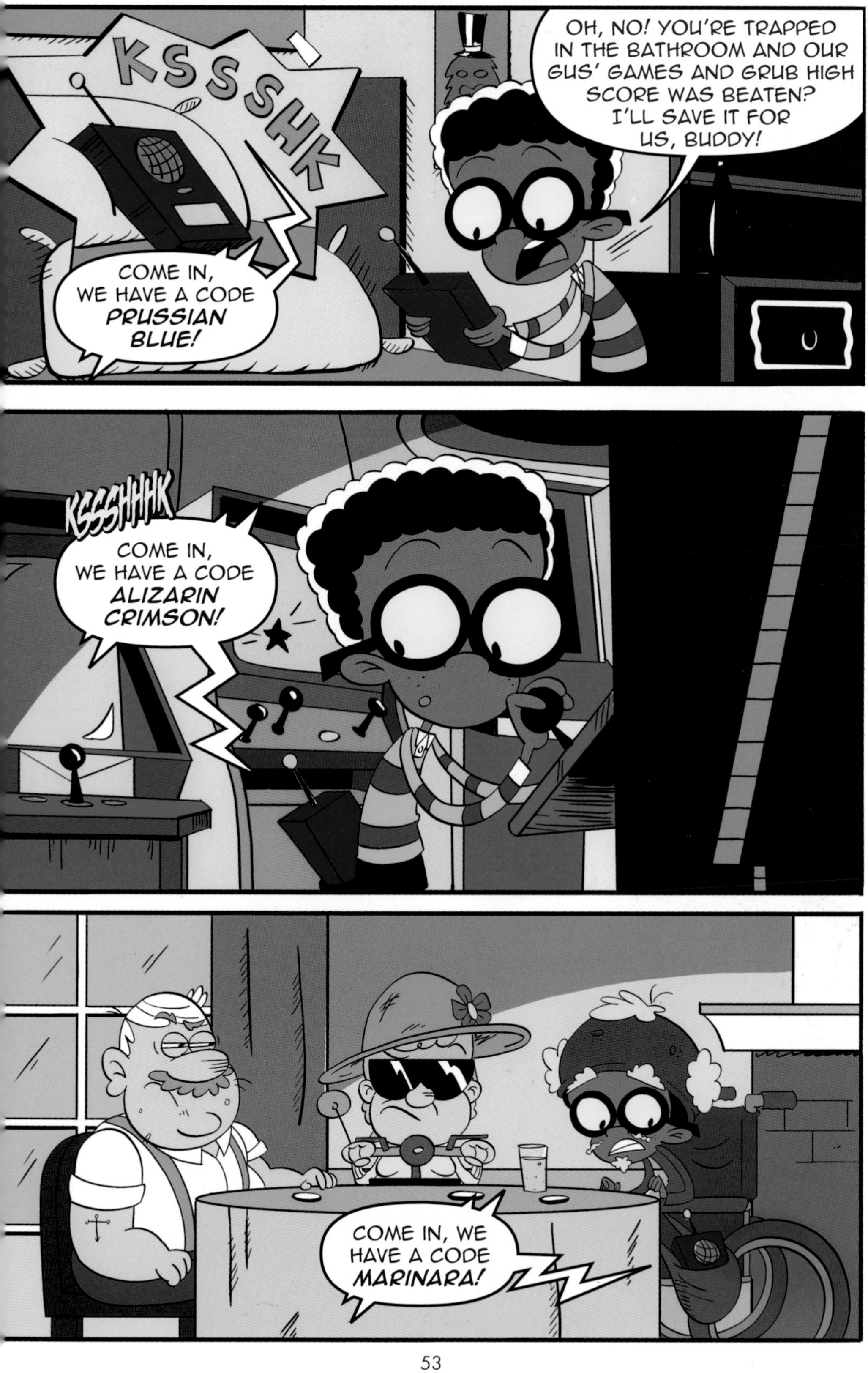
KSSSHK
OH, NO! YOU'RE TRAPPED IN THE BATHROOM AND OUR GUS' GAMES AND GRUB HIGH SCORE WAS BEATEN? I'LL SAVE IT FOR US, BUDDY!
COME IN, WE HAVE A CODE PRUSSIAN BLUE!
KSSSHHHK
COME IN, WE HAVE A CODE ALIZARIN CRIMSON!
COME IN, WE HAVE A CODE MARINARA!

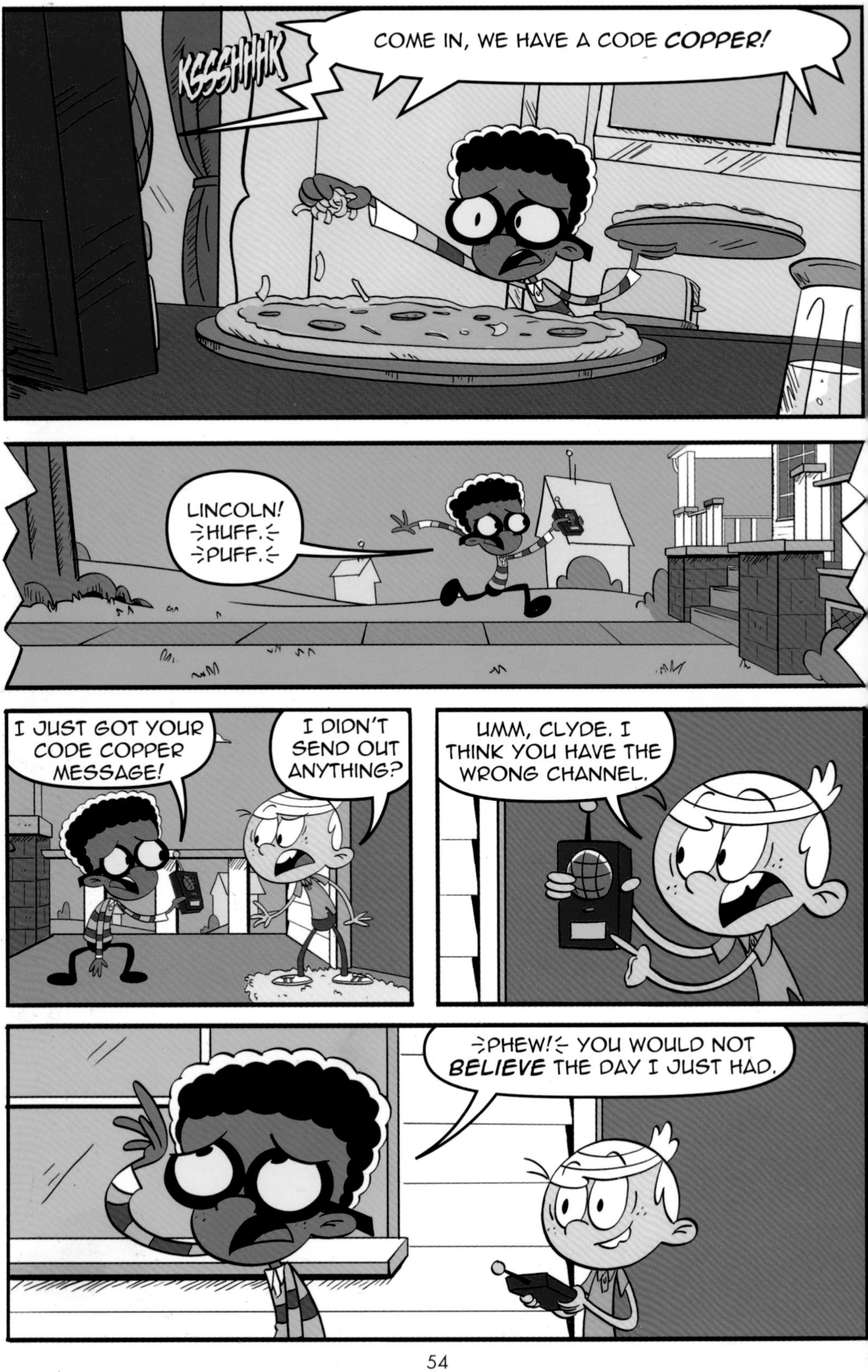
KSSSHHHK
COME IN, WE HAVE A CODE *COPPER!*
LINCOLN! HUFF. PUFF.
I JUST GOT YOUR CODE COPPER MESSAGE!
I DIDN'T SEND OUT ANYTHING?
UMM, CLYDE. I THINK YOU HAVE THE WRONG CHANNEL.
PHEW! YOU WOULD NOT *BELIEVE* THE DAY I JUST HAD.

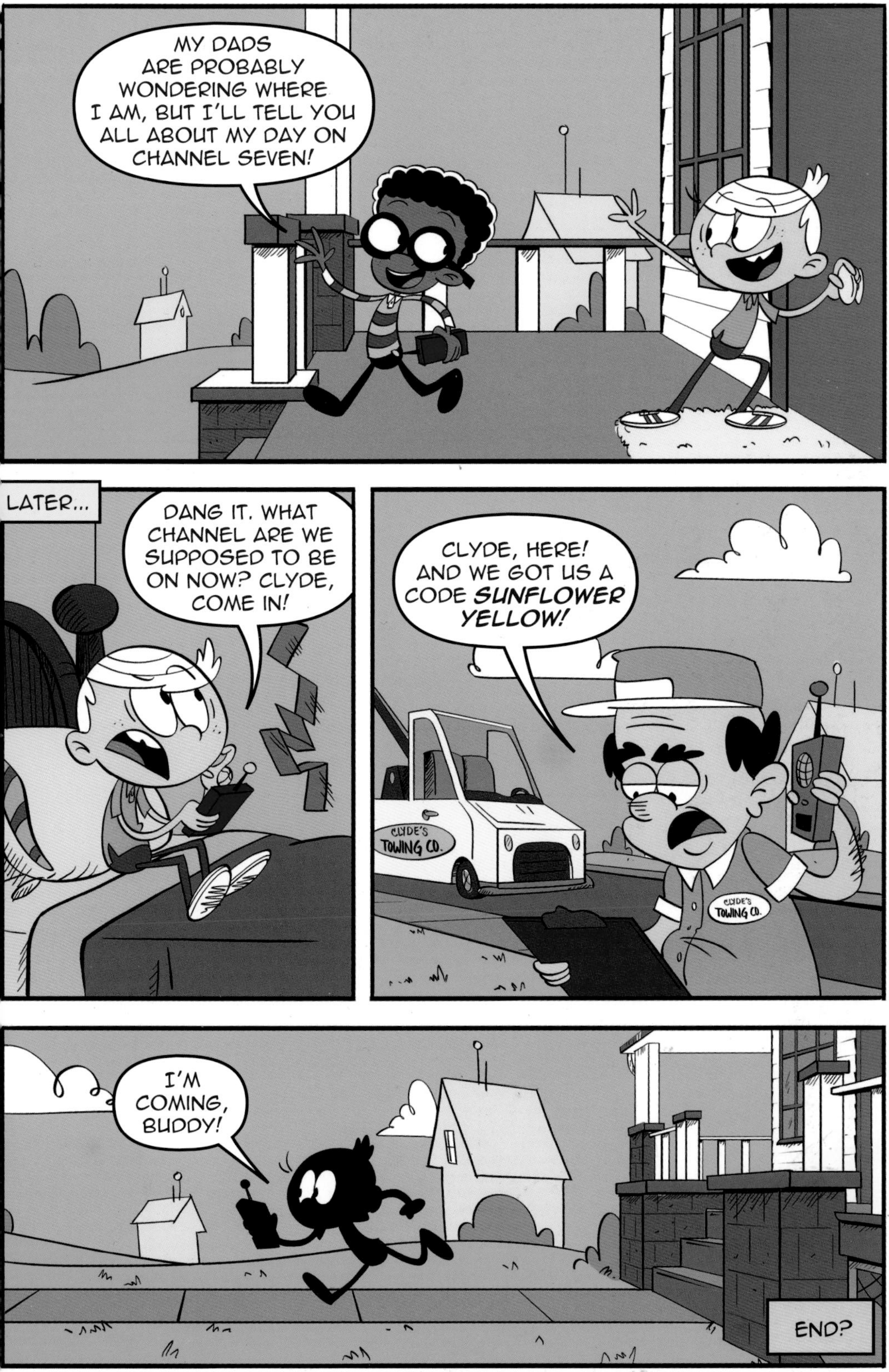
MY DADS ARE PROBABLY WONDERING WHERE I AM, BUT I'LL TELL YOU ALL ABOUT MY DAY ON CHANNEL SEVEN!
LATER...
DANG IT. WHAT CHANNEL ARE WE SUPPOSED TO BE ON NOW? CLYDE, COME IN!
CLYDE, HERE! AND WE GOT US A CODE SUNFLOWER YELLOW!
CLYDE'S TOWING CO.
CLYDE'S TOWING CO.
I'M COMING, BUDDY!
END?

WATCH OUT FOR PAPERCUTZ

Welcome to the sisters-surviving seventh, super-fun THE LOUD HOUSE graphic novel, "The Struggle is Real," from Papercutz – those hard-working residents of THE QUIET (publishing) HOUSE dedicated to publishing great graphic novels for all ages. I'm Jim Salicrup, Editor-in-Chief and Lily's Diaper-Changer, here with good news for those of you who just discovered that Papercutz is publishing THE LOUD HOUSE graphic novels...

But before we get to that, we just can't keep our mouths shut a moment longer about the really, really exciting news regarding THE LOUD HOUSE. We're just too excited! It was recently announced that Nickelodeon will be producing an original THE LOUD HOUSE animated movie for Netflix! That's right – a movie, featuring Lincoln Loud; his ten sisters, Lori, Leni, Luna, Luan, Lynn, Lucy, Lola, Lana, Lisa, and Lily; his parents, Rita and Lynn Sr.; their pets; and all their many friends! We haven't been this excited since we heard about that other upcoming THE LOUD HOUSE event, the new LOS CASAGRANDES series!

But back to THE LOUD HOUSE graphic novels... Since this is the seventh graphic novel of THE LOUD HOUSE, we're sure you've been able to deduce that there must have been six previous THE LOUD HOUSE graphic novels. That's 100% correct! If you've been picking them up at your favorite bookseller or library, and you already have all seven of the THE LOUD HOUSE, graphic novels then you're completely up-to-speed. But if you're just joining us, and feel a tad overwhelmed at having to find six previous graphic novels to enjoy all THE LOUD HOUSE comics that exist, we've got some good news to wipe away all your anxiety! Papercutz started a series of THE LOUD HOUSE 3 IN 1 graphic novels that collect three of the original graphic novels into one. So, you can find THE LOUD HOUSE #1-3 in THE LOUD HOUSE 3 IN 1 #1, and THE LOUD HOUSE #4-6 in (wait for it...) THE LOUD HOUSE 3 IN 1 #2! It's simply our way of trying to make life as easy as possible for you.

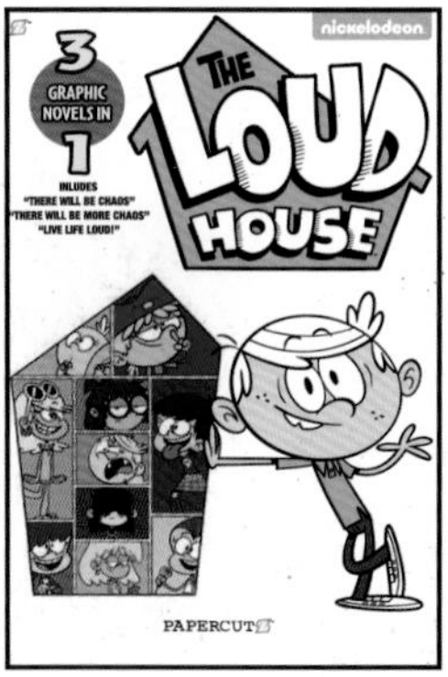
nickelodeon
3
GRAPHIC NOVELS IN
1
THE LOUD HOUSE
INCLUDES
"THERE WILL BE CHAOS"
"THERE WILL BE MORE CHAOS"
"LIVE LIFE LOUD!"
PAPERCUTZ

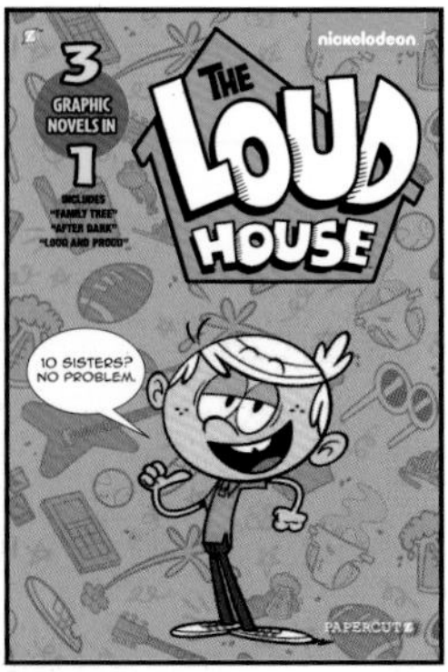
nickelodeon
3
GRAPHIC NOVELS IN
1
THE LOUD HOUSE
10 SISTERS? NO PROBLEM.
PAPERCUTZ

Of course, you can still get each of THE LOUD HOUSE graphic novels separately at your favorite booksellers. You can even get them digitally wherever e-books are sold – including at www.comiXology.com – if you prefer enjoying comics on your various digital devices. But if you're one of those completists, who absolutely must have each and every edition of THE LOUD HOUSE graphic novels, including second, third, and fourth printings, not to mention the mini-comic (which is re-presented on the following pages as a special bonus!) and the FREE COMIC BOOK DAY comic – we wish you luck! Trying to track down so many super-popular collector's item THE LOUD HOUSE graphic novels isn't easy! You could even say, "The Struggle is Real"! Collecting comics can be lots of fun – just ask Lincoln and Clyde – but we're trying to make getting THE LOUD HOUSE graphic novels as easy as possible. That's why you'll see THE LOUD HOUSE graphic novels popping up at more and more stores every day, not to mention book fairs, and even a few unexpected places.

Which is our cue, to remind that coming soon to a bookseller near you (possibly even at Flip's Food and Fuel, but be careful not to spill your Flippee on it!) is THE LOUD HOUSE #8 "Livin' la Casa Loud"! Not only will it feature all sorts of great comics starring your favorite characters from THE LOUD HOUSE, there's a very good chance there'll also be a Watch Out for Papercutz page with news about THE LOUD HOUSE #9! And we're sure you won't want to miss that!

Thanks, Jim

STAY IN TOUCH!

EMAIL:	salicrup@papercutz.com
WEB:	papercutz.com
TWITTER:	@papercutzgn
INSTAGRAM:	@papercutzgn
FACEBOOK:	PAPERCUTZGRAPHICNOVELS
FANMAIL:	Papercutz, 160 Broadway, Suite 700, East Wing, New York, NY 10038

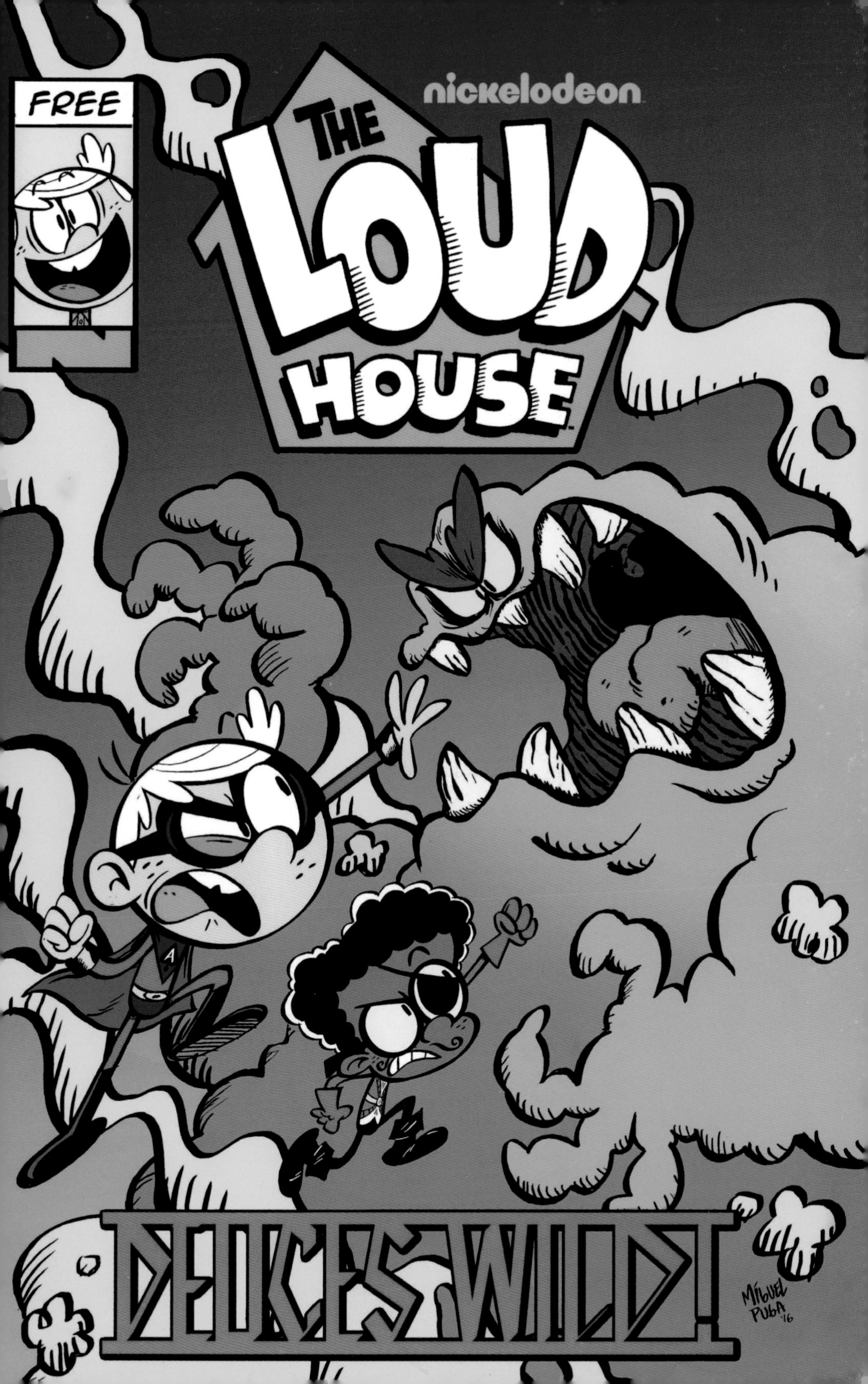
FREE
nickelodeon
THE LOUD HOUSE
DEUCES WILD!
MIGUEL PUGA '16

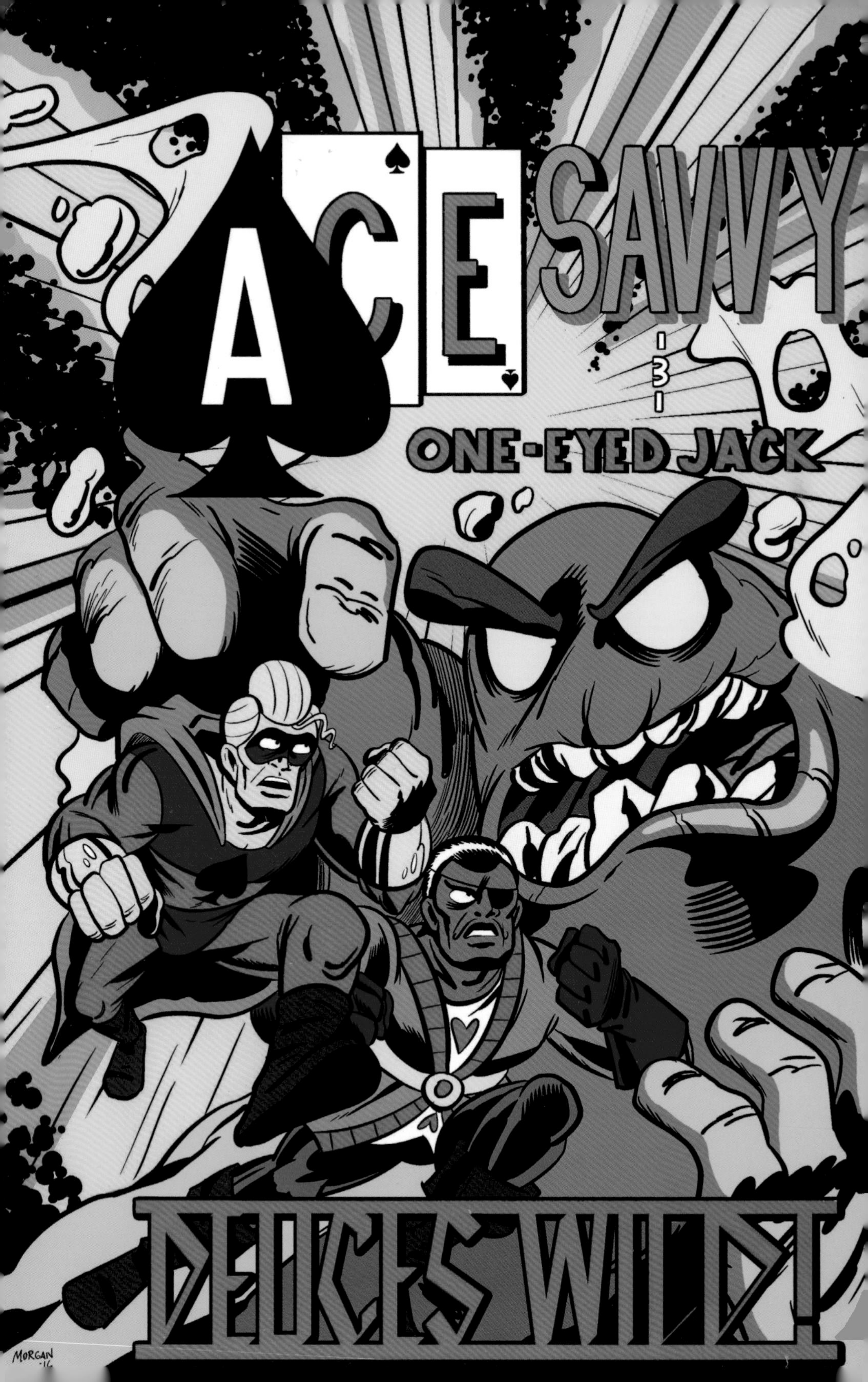
ACE SAVVY
3
ONE-EYED JACK
DEUCES WILD!
MORGAN '16

"DEUCES WILD"

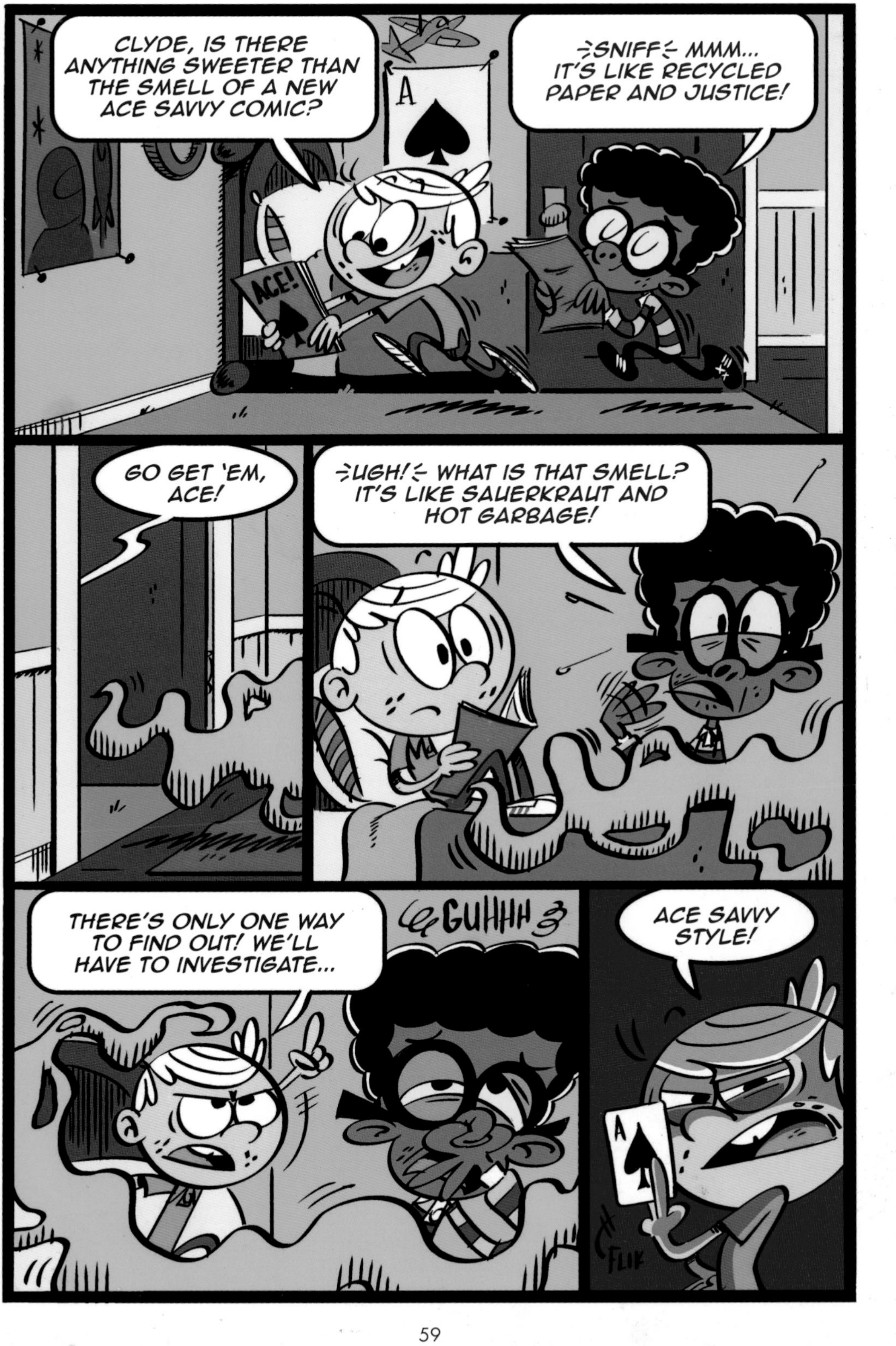
CLYDE, IS THERE ANYTHING SWEETER THAN THE SMELL OF A NEW ACE SAVVY COMIC?
SNIFF MMM... IT'S LIKE RECYCLED PAPER AND JUSTICE!
ACE!
GO GET 'EM, ACE!
UGH! WHAT IS THAT SMELL? IT'S LIKE SAUERKRAUT AND HOT GARBAGE!
THERE'S ONLY ONE WAY TO FIND OUT! WE'LL HAVE TO INVESTIGATE...
GUHHH
ACE SAVVY STYLE!
FLIK

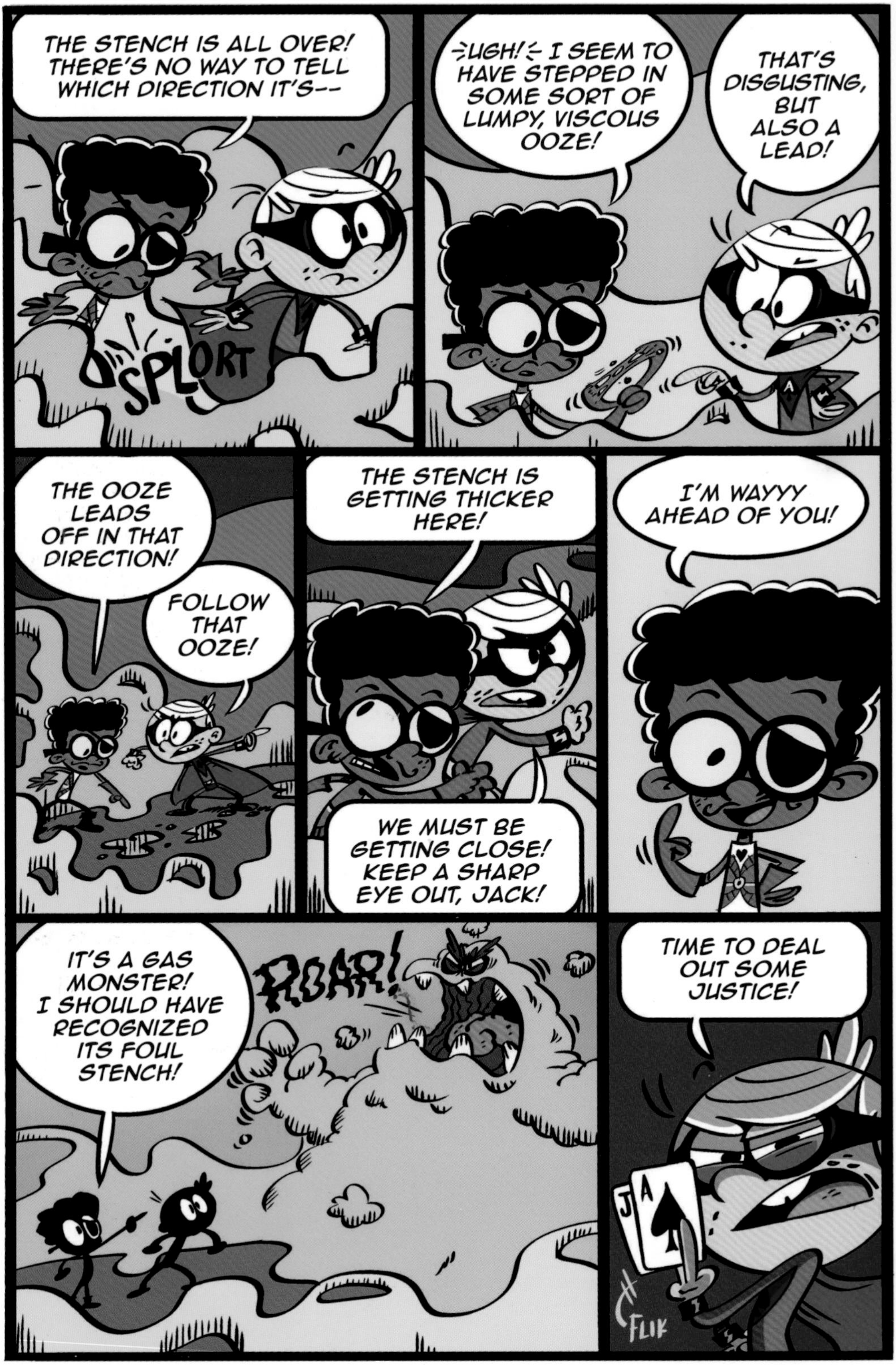
THE STENCH IS ALL OVER! THERE'S NO WAY TO TELL WHICH DIRECTION IT'S--
SPLORT
UGH! I SEEM TO HAVE STEPPED IN SOME SORT OF LUMPY, VISCOUS OOZE!
THAT'S DISGUSTING, BUT ALSO A LEAD!
THE OOZE LEADS OFF IN THAT DIRECTION!
FOLLOW THAT OOZE!
THE STENCH IS GETTING THICKER HERE!
WE MUST BE GETTING CLOSE! KEEP A SHARP EYE OUT, JACK!
I'M WAYYY AHEAD OF YOU!
IT'S A GAS MONSTER! I SHOULD HAVE RECOGNIZED ITS FOUL STENCH!
ROAR!
TIME TO DEAL OUT SOME JUSTICE!
FLIK

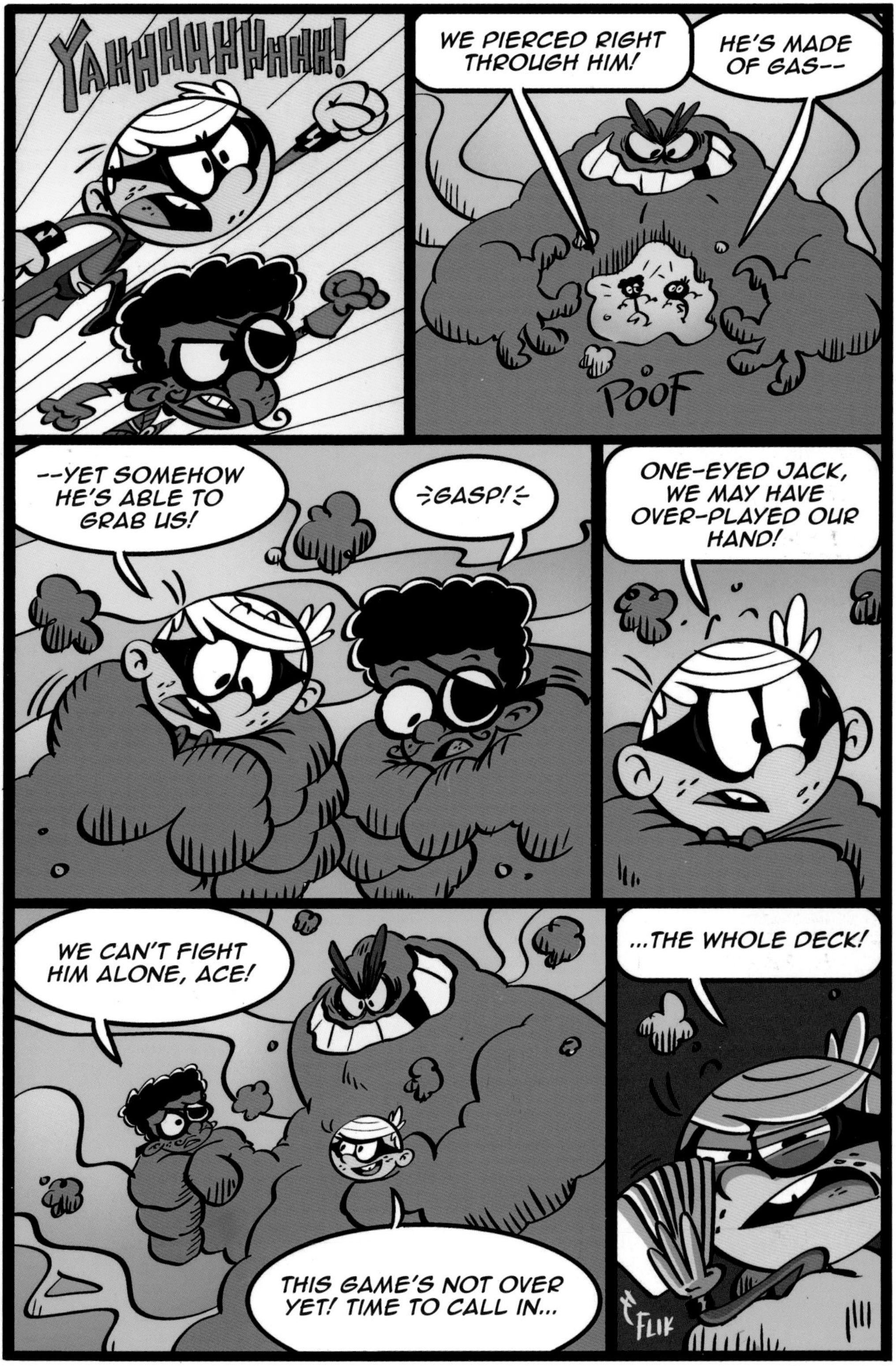
YAHHHHHHHHH!
WE PIERCED RIGHT THROUGH HIM!
HE'S MADE OF GAS--
POOF
--YET SOMEHOW HE'S ABLE TO GRAB US!
GASP!
ONE-EYED JACK, WE MAY HAVE OVER-PLAYED OUR HAND!
WE CAN'T FIGHT HIM ALONE, ACE!
THIS GAME'S NOT OVER YET! TIME TO CALL IN...
...THE WHOLE DECK!
FLIK

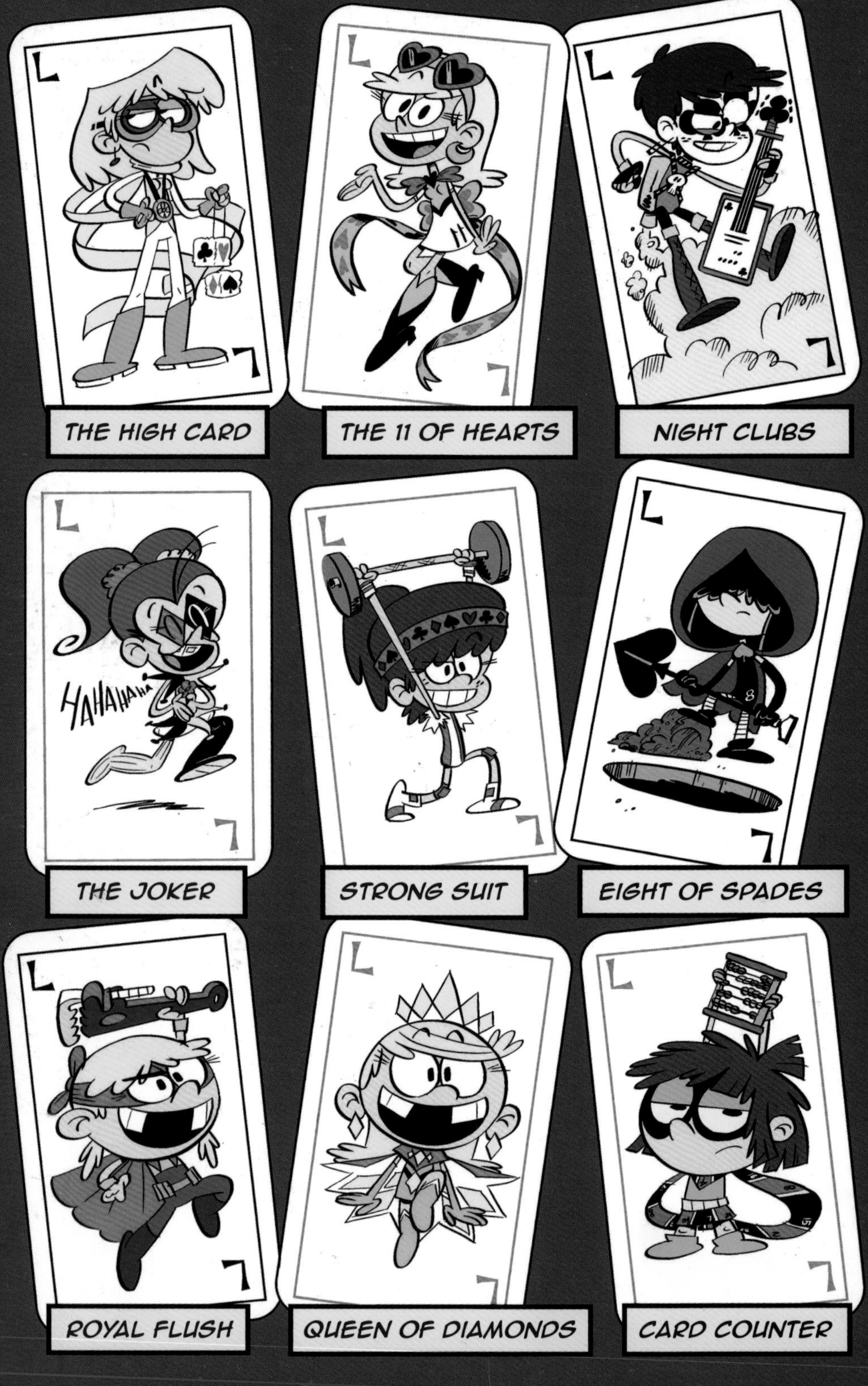
THE HIGH CARD
THE 11 OF HEARTS
NIGHT CLUBS
HAHAHAHA
THE JOKER
STRONG SUIT
EIGHT OF SPADES
ROYAL FLUSH
QUEEN OF DIAMONDS
CARD COUNTER

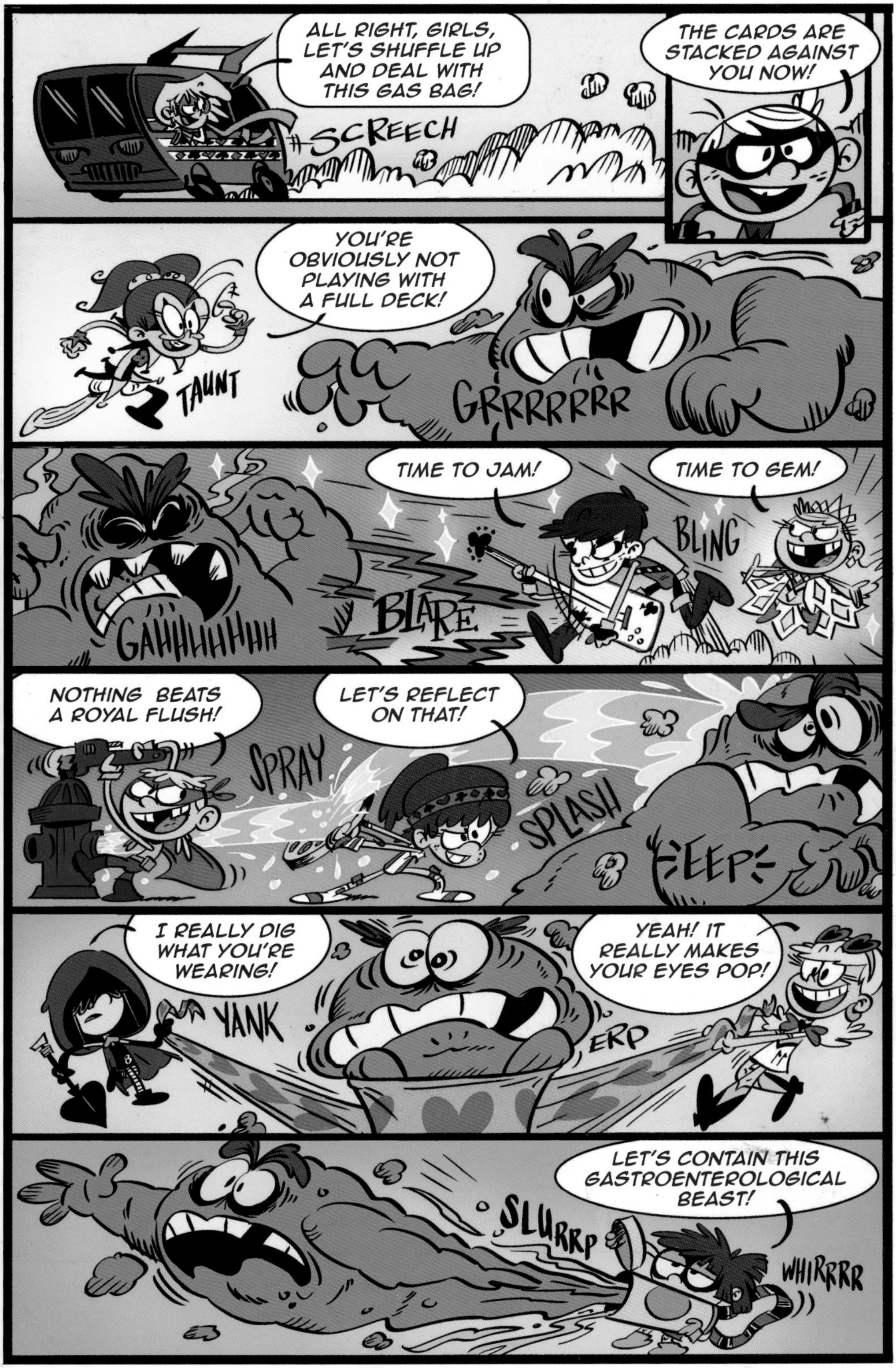
ALL RIGHT, GIRLS, LET'S SHUFFLE UP AND DEAL WITH THIS GAS BAG!
SCREECH
THE CARDS ARE STACKED AGAINST YOU NOW!
YOU'RE OBVIOUSLY NOT PLAYING WITH A FULL DECK!
TAUNT
GRRRRRRR
TIME TO JAM!
TIME TO GEM!
BLING
BLARE
GAHHHHHHH
NOTHING BEATS A ROYAL FLUSH!
LET'S REFLECT ON THAT!
SPRAY
SPLASH
EEP
I REALLY DIG WHAT YOU'RE WEARING!
YEAH! IT REALLY MAKES YOUR EYES POP!
YANK
ERP
LET'S CONTAIN THIS GASTROENTEROLOGICAL BEAST!
SLURRP
WHIRRRR

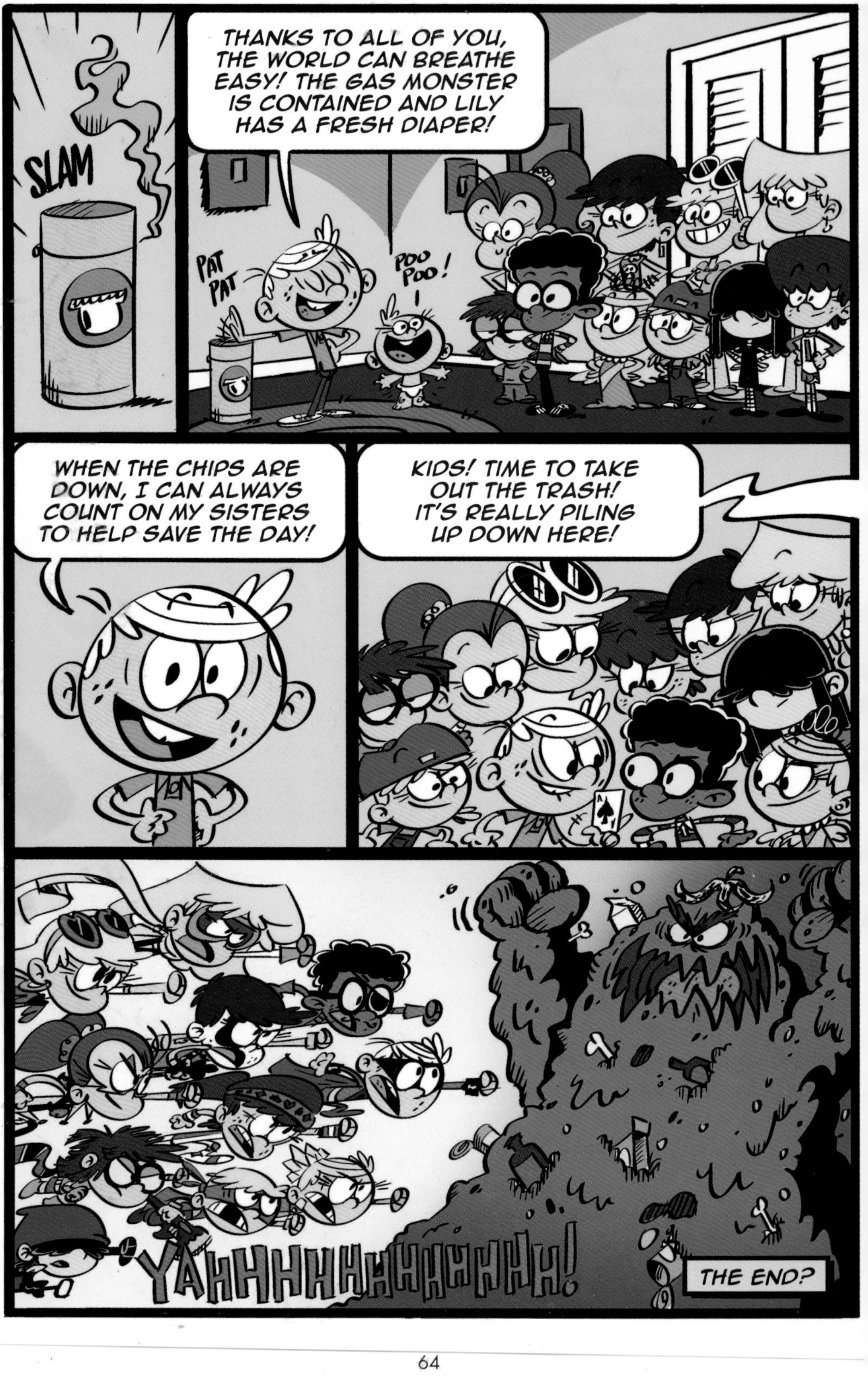
SLAM
THANKS TO ALL OF YOU, THE WORLD CAN BREATHE EASY! THE GAS MONSTER IS CONTAINED AND LILY HAS A FRESH DIAPER!
PAT PAT
POO POO!
WHEN THE CHIPS ARE DOWN, I CAN ALWAYS COUNT ON MY SISTERS TO HELP SAVE THE DAY!
KIDS! TIME TO TAKE OUT THE TRASH! IT'S REALLY PILING UP DOWN HERE!
YAHHHHHHHHHHHHH!
THE END?